Sonahchi

Sonahchi

A Collection of Myth-Tales
by PAT CARR

CINCO PUNTOS PRESS EL PASO, TEXAS

ACKNOWLEDGEMENTS

Grateful acknowledgement is given to the following publications in which a number of these stories first appeared: *Writers' Forum 5* ("Buffalo Man"), *La Confluencia* ("The Emergence"), *Cedar Rock* ("Atocle Woman"), *Puerto del Sol* ("The Corn Maidens"), *The Human Crowd: New Fiction from the Minnesota Review* ("Baholikonga"), *Coyote's Journal* ("Coyote's Wager"), and *The River City Review* ("The Frog Husband").

ISBN 0-938317-06-7
Library of Congress Catalog Card Number: 88-70067

FIRST EDITION
2nd Printing

Cinco Puntos Press would like to thank Twelve Trees Press of Pasadena, California, for permission to use a reproduction from *Within The Underworld Sky, Mimbres Ceramic Art In Context* (1984) by Barbara Moulard in the design of *Sonahchi*. The pot from which the design is taken is a Mimbres Boldfaced Black-on-white hemispheric vessel (ca. AD 800-1000). The original photograph is by John Bigelow Taylor.

CONTENTS

PREFACE

A FEW years ago when I was researching Pueblo Indian tales for my work on the mythology of Mimbres pottery, I found myself responding to certain of the stories because they seemed to me to deal with the basic human conflicts and experiences—love, death, birth, jealousy, betrayal—in short, all those archetypal themes dealt with in world literature. Many of the plots and characters of these ancient Indian tales seemed well suited for a more contemporary treatment, and I found myself recreating them as my own stories.

The following myth-tales are the result.

PAT CARR
1988

And the storyteller
raised a hand and began, "Sonahchi.
Well, then, at the beginning...."

THE EMERGENCE

*The people were unhappy
in the dark and
crowded underworld.
Sun took pity on their misery.*
—OLD PUEBLO MYTH

SHE knew they had to go, but this time she wanted to stay. Their baby lay flexed beneath the adobe floor of the house, close to her, to them, and it was too hard, too uncaring and unloving, to leave his little body alone as they moved on again. She must not go. The tiny food bowl she had coiled and painted to fit over his little skull had a locust drawn in the center, his favorite insect, one he had caught twice with his baby laughter and pudgy dimpled hand when he had been warm and alive. The fat little hands that she had crossed over his chest as they put him....

The thought of going away without the baby was unbearable.

"But we must go," he said behind her and laid his hands on her shoulders as if he knew what was in her mind. "They have told us we must all go." He put his face into the side of her neck. "We will be together, and we will have another son when we get to the new home. We will never forget our first born, and that is what is important."

1

"He will be left alone beneath the hardened mud with no family beside him. No other brothers, not his mother or father. I have the bowls ready, painted for our own burial when we go to join him," she said stubbornly.

He shook his head. "We must leave the bowls behind. They have said we cannot take anything with us."

"What of the metates for grinding? The polishing stones?"

"We will get others in the new home."

She could tell from his tone that he was finished, that he would argue to convince her no more, and she knew that she would go with him.

She looked up and the world roof was dark and overcast. It would rain again before they left and the mud would slide beneath their feet, sucking at their ankles, holding them back.

She went down the ladder into the single room of the house and knelt beside the wall close to where the baby was buried. She sat quiet, not speaking to the little body beneath the floor, merely being close to him until it was time to go. As she waited, she could hear the first spatters of rain on the outside wall.

Then, before she was ready, he called down to her over the pounding of the rain. "We must leave now." He watched her, sheltering his forehead against the waters that had soaked his hair, and without speaking, she went up the ladder to join him.

He always seemed to understand, and he took her hand and pressed it.

They went to stand with the others who had collected in the mud that splashed and oozed around them, and they listened through the heavy rain to the instructions of the bow priests and the caciques who would lead.

She held his hand as all of the people formed into a long, silent line that spread down the muddy hill, past the pueblos of the village, down into the valley itself. She had not thought their village had held so many people.

They waited without talking, the long patient line of the people, even the children quiet, not whimpering or crying, as the rain streamed over them, turning the black clay mud into thick black liquid.

She looked at their house where they had been happy with the baby and where the tiny child lay beneath his sheltering bowl. But as the line moved slowly ahead, the house was lost to her view in the gray shroud of water.

Then it was her turn, and he lifted her slightly out of the mud and held her against his chest until her feet and hands caught at the first rungs.

"Do not look back. I am here behind you."

The rungs were harsh, crudely and quickly hewn of cane, and even the scores of hands that had touched them before her had not smoothed the many points of cane splinters.

She was not as strong as she had been before the death of the baby and she could feel her arms getting heavy too soon, her breath pulling sharp against her lungs too soon. But the rain had stopped, or at least she, they, were sheltered from it, and the rungs were slippery only with the mud that the others ahead of her had left.

She paused to rest, but he stroked her calf from below and said quietly, "We cannot wait. There are too many others behind us, and we must go on. It is only a little further."

Of course it was much, much further, and they both knew it, but she started again. She had never wanted to come, but they would be together and they would begin a new life in the new home. That thought had to be enough, had to keep her going. And she climbed, kept climbing for what seemed hours longer, hanging onto the cane, holding it tight with aching palms, aching soles that pressed heavily against the curve of the wood.

She moved her arms and legs by sheer force of will as the hours passed.

Perhaps the caciques and the bow priests had been mistaken and they would find nothing. Perhaps they had been deliberately misled and the people would merely climb without ceasing, without ever....

"Listen," he said suddenly behind her. And as she raised one arm and then the other, she could hear it. A sound like no other she had ever heard. A singing, yet not a singing of the people. A small clear song without words, joyful, beckoning, brimming with triumphant notes that flowed, trilled, then broke loose from their arch of sound to shower down over them.

"And see," he said, his voice excited. "There! Straight above. It must be the Sun of which the bow priests knew."

She looked up as she climbed, and there was a luminous brightness made of a color that chipped into many colors and scattered into writhing, wriggling bits of light about the opening she could see.

"We are almost there!" he said exultant behind her.

The opening came closer, revealed a great vastness beyond as she reached for rung after rung. The brightness swayed dizzily, fragmenting, weaving, untangling its mingled colors as the figures just ahead of her alternately blocked and disclosed it.

At last she was at the opening. A hand reached for hers and pulled her up.

The terrible brightness was blinding and she cried out with the pain in her eyes, her temples. She clapped her free hand over her eyes and felt the involuntary pain-water seep through the lids.

"Welcome to the Fourth World," a voice said heartily, husky from having said the phrase so many times.

She was drawn free of the ladder and placed on her feet, but she dropped to her knees in the pain, unable to open her eyes.

Suddenly a silence enveloped her, sprang around her, as the sound, the joyous clear clean song abruptly stopped.

"Ah, the song of the Mockingbird has ended," the voice said. "No more of the people can come out of the sipapu."

She forced her eyes open, and through the haze of tears that stood in them she could see his arm aloft at the opening.

"No! No!" She threw herself back toward the hole that was shrinking, closing.

Her hand grasped at his, their fingers and the webs between their fingers clinging, clutching briefly before his hand slid away, down, and the sides of the sipapu clamped tight around her arm.

"No! No!" Her eyes shut themselves again.

"Come, come," the same hearty, hoarse voice said above her as a hand drew her arm carefully from the miniature opening and patted her shoulder.

"Come, open your eyes and enjoy this new world. Everything is beautiful. See. Even where your eyes water the ground with the first ache of our Sun a beautiful buttercup springs. See," the voice said happily and the hand patted her again in her darkness.

THE CORN MAIDENS

The Corn Maidens were the mothers of men.
They gave of their flesh that the people might have food.
But when the people used the corn carelessly,
the Corn Maidens were resentful
and went away to a distant land.
—ANCIENT ZUÑI MYTH

SHE'D seen him in the brake beside the pool, waiting for an antelope to come, waiting, leaning against the rock where she sat to dry her hair after rinsing out the yucca suds.

He was to her like the antelope he'd come to snare, his skin smooth, the muscles knotted beneath its glistening and his shirt, his hair contained by a scarlet headband. As he tensed at her step, his weapon ready, their eyes met.

He'd turned away first and had dropped down beside the stone, her stone.

She'd waited, her sandals planted in the damp sand at the rim of the water, but he crouched low, silent, and didn't reappear. At last she too had turned away with her vase of water and had gone back to the adobe house.

"I've seen a man," she said to Blue Corn Girl as she came down the ladder.

"Oh?" Blue Corn Girl didn't look up from her grinding stone and her meal that was beginning to turn into a soft pile of lavender blue dust. No one could grind corn any finer than Blue Corn Girl.

"Down by the pool waiting for an antelope."

"Then he was a human?"

Yellow Corn Girl nodded. "Yes. He was a human."

Blue Corn Girl still didn't look up. "I can't remember how many years it's been since I last saw a human being." She scooped the pale lavender powder into a basket and poured another handful of coarser, but still fine, meal into the metate.

"The land used to be crowded with them, but you are much younger than I and probably don't remember many of them." Yellow Corn Girl didn't know why she felt compelled to remind her sister just then that she was the elder.

"Is this one any different than the others?" The mano twisted and circled and crushed still finer the already cracked blue kernels.

"No."

"I think I'd still like to see this one. It's been so long," Blue Corn Girl said.

"Perhaps he'll be there tomorrow when you go for water," Yellow Corn Girl said, her voice casual.

"Perhaps."

The next morning, however, as Blue Corn Girl plaited everyday turkey feathers in her hair and dressed in her everyday dark blanket, she seemed to have forgotten the man. "I'll bring the water and some cattails if any are plump and ripe," she said as she went up the ladder.

Yellow Corn Girl was already at her grinding.

The man had been wearing a shirt the color of the sky, she remembered, and his flesh had shimmered at the V of his collar.

She remembered his slender hand on his weapon, his movements sleek as an animal. She ground the yellow corn, brushed it into a woven tray, ground again, and she remembered all day.

All day until the sky turned from the white of noon to the rose of twilight and finally into the speckled black of night, and still Blue Corn Girl did not return.

Yellow Corn Girl couldn't sleep and lay in her blanket staring at the square of night above her in the roof. It was always the same. She should have known it would always be the same.

Morning came, but she didn't go up the ladder into the day. She could wait in the house for Blue Corn Girl.

Other mornings and other nights came before Blue Corn Girl returned, but at last she climbed back down the ladder.

"Where have you been?" Yellow Corn Girl asked as her sister began to take down her hair whorls. She no longer had them braided with turkey feathers.

"With the man."

"Oh?"

"Yes. He is very nice." She looked back at the entrance as if she had heard something, someone, on the roof. "He's coming for me this afternoon."

Yellow Corn Girl nodded. "I shall go with you."

Blue Corn Girl glanced at her and sighed. "I shall wear my blanket with the butterfly weaving and my turquoise pendants."

Yellow Corn Girl nodded again and got the things down from their shelf in the adobe wall. And when Blue Corn Girl was dressed, they climbed back up the ladder.

"Where are you to meet the man?"

"At the pool."

They walked together, their sandals leaving no imprint on the hard dry earth that had cracked into great fissures beneath the white sun.

"There he is." Blue Corn Girl nodded toward him.

"Yes."

He was standing near an old blue pick-up, and Yellow Corn Girl could see that he was slender and tall. He was still wearing a blue jean shirt, but now it was unbuttoned far down his chest and was tucked into blue jean trousers.

"His hair is the color of corn silk," Blue Corn Girl said.

"Yes."

It was true. Long gold corn silk held back from his forehead with the scarlet headband, and eyes of dark, dark blue.

He came to meet them and Yellow Corn Girl saw that he walked light and graceful, young and strong. He was watching only Blue Corn Girl.

She let Blue Corn Girl go forward toward him as she went to the pick-up.

The rifle she'd seen in his hands by the pool was lying in the pick-up bed and she lifted it out as he stopped beside her sister.

Blue Corn Girl glanced at her as she aimed the gun and she saw Blue Corn Girl's head shake slightly.

The man must have seen something in Blue Corn Girl's eyes, and he started to turn as Yellow Corn Girl pulled the trigger. The bullet hit him in the temple rather than behind the ear as she'd intended.

His long slender legs bent and he slid over them to the ground as though his body had been dumped from a tray. His head struck the hard baked earth and his blond hair fanned out almost to the toe of Blue Corn Girl's sandal.

She sighed, looked down at him and back up at Yellow Corn Girl. "Must it always be this way?"

It always was. From the time the first men came with the atlatl to hunt the sacred antelope and then with the bow and arrow and now with the rifle. All the Indians and now the anglos. All falling in love with Blue Corn Girl.

"An immortal can never keep a human being for very long. They always change and fade and then wither into salt dust," she said. "It is better to hold the memory of one of them, remembering him beside a rock, that moment when your eyes met for the first and last time."

BUFFALO MAN

When buffaloes are in their own country,
they seem like people.
When they are away from their own land,
they are just like buffaloes.
—JICARILLA APACHE MYTH

AFTER the third day she knew it was too late to go back even if she'd wanted to. They would have found her things, the trail of the herd, and her husband would have started after her. But perhaps he would give up before he found them. They traveled so fast and went so far each day.

By day she rode on his back just behind the great hump that she clung to, her fingers tangled in his shaggy hair, her body bent forward against the wind.

At night when the herd paused, he took his man shape and came to her in the gleaming white buckskin with turquoise necklaces and made love to her strong and fierce in the shelter of buffalo robes. And as they lay together after the lovemaking, she tangled her fingers in his curling hair, explored his chest with her palm, marveling that curling hair grew there too.

After a week they stopped in a valley, encamping to let the cows calve before they moved on, and she was able to gather long reeds to weave new water baskets, a large-mouthed one for him to use in the day, a narrow-lipped one for the two of them after dark.

They had come so far from her pueblo land, and she wondered at the cliffed blue mountains, the tall grasses, the pine trees that stretched on and on, full of golden resin to caulk her water baskets.

9

"Are you happy here in the grass land?" he asked in the evening after they had made love and he was holding her close beneath the buffalo robes.

"I think perhaps every woman wants more than anything in her life to be held like this."

He turned his head slightly to smile at her, his arms tightening, and she relaxed against the hair on his chest, wishing that she could merge with, into, his flesh, his bone, that they could never be separated.

And when she realized that she was going to have his child, she thought that possibly her husband had already given up.

She ran out to the valley where the herd wandered lazily, munching the dew-strung grasses that came as high as her knees. She saw him near the ridge, standing, looking down on the others. He was so beautiful, and she paused for a moment to watch his shoulders, his powerful head, the horns that looked like polished shell in the morning light. Then she ran to him, feeling the dew splash like pond water on her ankles.

She flung herself against his massive shoulder, but he was so strong her weight didn't even make him flinch.

He turned to watch her, and she saw his great eyes soften.

She stroked his head. "I am with child," she said softly.

He muzzled her and she leaned against him.

"I know it will be a son."

He gazed at her, his eyes dark and liquid.

She laughed, hugged him, as much of him as she could reach, and filled her lungs with the morning air and the smell of his wool.

That evening as the white bone sliver of moon swung from the black night, he came into the buffalo robe shelter with a rabbit he'd killed with his hooves just at dusk.

"I knew you liked meat sometimes," he said as he held it up for her. "You must eat well for our son."

She laughed and showed him how to skin it with her flint knife, how to cook it in the woven basket with hot stones from the fire that made the water boil.

When the pieces of rabbit were cooked, however, she couldn't get him to taste the meat. But he watched her eat and they laughed at everything.

In the morning she awoke, dressed quickly, and braided a length of red vine in her hair, knowing he liked red.

But as she came to the valley, she saw the pony, and she knew.

And when she reached the little hillock cresting the valley, she could see her husband standing over him, the arrows, many arrows, in his side. She knew he was dead before she came close to him.

"I followed the tracks," her husband said. "Even after the others had given up, I followed." There was a touch of pride in his voice. Then, "He is the one who carried you away?"

She nodded mutely. It would of course have taken many arrows.

"He abducted you, didn't he?"

She felt his little eyes narrowed toward her, but she didn't look at him as she nodded again.

"Well, then," he said, but still she didn't look at him. He waited and when she said nothing, he added, "We shall start back. I have left the corn too long already in this search."

He started to take his flint knife from the sheath at his waist. "There is much meat here, but I'll cut off only the tongue. We can roast it on the way to the pueblo, and it will last us many days."

"No," she said and crossed quickly between them.

She dropped to her knees and lifted the great head onto her lap. It was even heavier than she'd expected, and there was a streak of drying blood at the corner of the mouth. She wiped at it with her palm.

Her husband stopped and for the first time she raised her head and looked at him.

"You went with him willingly," he said, his voice like a branch in winter. "You loved him."

She stared at him full in the face and nodded.

With cold deliberation he pulled an arrow from the quiver she had made for him and set it to the bow. She watched his arm pull back. How thin his arms looked, how lank and stiff his straight hair.

The arrow hit her in the throat, but there was no pain. It was only as if something had tightened around her neck and was shutting off her breath, her words.

But she didn't need words. She leaned slowly forward around the shaft of the arrow to cradle his head in her arms, to feel the soft curls of his wool in her hands.

SPIDER WOMAN

Far away at Kunluokyut'e'e
the Little War Twins were living.
They had no mother or father,
only a grandmother.
—OLD TEWA MYTH

SHE looked around her little room and smiled with satisfaction. All of her materials were in a proper order; everything was in place, everything was folded, stacked, balanced, hung in its correct niche. She couldn't remember that the cooking utensils had ever been so neatly straight in all the years the children had been at home.

She went over to the weaving poles and sat down gingerly, bending her stiff knee under her with slow easements as she flexed her hands, massaged the joint of her thumb. She couldn't remember either when her thumb hadn't ached on cold mornings, but that was merely a part of growing old. The fragile silence of her empty rooms that allowed her to distinguish the delicate clicking of frozen grass in the night and the whisper of snow in the dawn more than compensated for the spidery appearance of feebleness and old age.

As she pressed the pain out of the thumb and its socket, she gazed gravely at the nearly finished weaving on the loom. A new design in dazzling white so vibrant and bold that it seemed almost violent, and she knew that when she took the completed work into the sun, the snowy warp and selvedge would appear almost crystalline. None of her children or her grandchildren would have liked it. They would have considered it unbecoming for a woman of her age to play with such startling patterns, but she no longer had to please them, any of them, and the angry slicing of the white strands across each other gave her great pleasure.

As did the quiet to work without explaining or reminding or reprimanding.

She smiled again and picked up her shuttle. Weaving took a certain concentration, and the peace around her at last allowed for the conception of designs she'd never envisioned before.

"I have come," a voice called down.

"You are welcome, daughter," she answered automatically, but she didn't recognize the young woman's voice.

A young girl, not quite a woman, climbed awkwardly down into the room with a heavy bundle in her arms. She looked at the newly spun threads drying on the racks, at the new weaving on the loom poles, then at Spider Woman herself. "You are Spider Grandmother?"

Spider Woman winced. She'd never liked that name. It made old women so facelessly the same. But she nodded at the stranger. "Would you like food?"

"I am very hungry and tired." And the girl-woman sank down where she stood, crumbling, folding over her large and obviously weighty package as though she'd been keeping herself upright by will alone.

Spider Woman built up the little fire again, and it popped, spat out a thin transparent smoke.

She glanced occasionally at the young woman as she worked, but the woman had dropped her head back and had closed her eyes. She still grasped the bundle tight in her arms as if afraid Spider Woman might peek inside.

Spider Woman felt her mouth clamp with irritation, felt the webbing age lines deepen around her lips. The woman certainly had nothing to worry about there. She had absolutely no interest in what was in the bundle. Some precious trade goods that made the girl-woman—she seemed hardly more than a child as she leaned there with her mouth slightly ajar and her treasure clutched against her chest—so tired and hungry. Well, if there was anything she, Spider Woman, had already too much of, it was trade goods. And if the child was afraid she might ask for some bit of trash in payment for hospitality and food, well....

The young woman didn't open her eyes again until Spider Woman put the warmed meal before her and shook her arm. Then she looked around, slightly dazed, then alarmed, as she carefully edged the packet down beside her.

It immediately began to move.

The young woman didn't seem to notice as she began greedily stuffing the inexhaustible supply of food into her mouth, not observing ceremony or politeness.

The wrapping of the package wriggled, writhed, squirmed.

Finally it parted, and a tiny fist poked out. The aimlessly thrashing hand was the color of sunset.

"You have a newborn, daughter?"

The young woman looked up, her mouth full of the corn balls, and nodded. She reached over and drew back the rest of the cover, exposing two little puckered faces, two pairs of grabbing fists.

"Twins!"

The girl nodded again. "That is why I have come to you, Spider Grandmother. You have lived a long while and are wise and know how to deal with many things that others have no knowledge of."

Spider Woman moved closer. "I have never seen twins."

The young woman was wiping her fingers on her skirt. "If I try to keep them, they will be put to death by my clan."

Spider Woman shook her head sympathetically. She knew the superstitions, the cases they could cite of terrible disasters caused by the birth of twins. She kept looking down at the pair of babies, not sure if she felt more sympathy for the girl's terrified people or for the two tiny forms in the bundle. Twins were indeed a frightening concept.

"That is why I am here," the young woman said once more as if that explained everything.

Spider Woman looked at her.

"You're not of my people, child."

"No, Spider Grandmother, and the bad luck won't follow them here." She glanced around again at the clean and tidy house. "If I leave them here with you, they'll be safe."

Spider Woman's thumb began to ache with a cold that seemed to spread from inside. Her breath had stopped at the entrance to her throat. "I am old, daughter, and I cannot keep your children."

The young woman searched her face. Then she said softly, "I have nowhere else to go, grandmother. You must take them."

Her mouth pursed itself again. "I cannot take them."

"They are twin boys. I have called them only Elder Brother and Younger Brother since this one was born first." She touched one baby forehead. "But you can give them other names."

Spider Woman didn't say anything.

"They were born in the woods. I was all alone and I gave birth to the pair of them by myself." A hint of pride had crept into her voice. "They came into the world in the dawning mist on Corn Mountain, and I knew when I saw that there were two that they were children of the Sun."

Just then the one on the right, the one who did seem possibly younger and slightly smaller than the other, turned his head and gave one of the unconscious, yet knowing, smiles of the newborn. His eyes opened with the smile, and he seemed to focus momentarily on Spider Woman.

Spider Woman heard her own voice saying to White Shell Woman, her own voice weighted with certainty, "Each child is everyone's child," and she shivered with a sudden chill that she hadn't noticed in the house before.

"I cannot return to my pueblo with them or they'll die," the young woman said again.

"I am an old woman who has lived alone too long."

"And I cannot leave them in the desert or in the woods or they'll be eaten. They're so tiny."

The baby grin on Younger Brother gleamed, sparkled wetly once more.

Spider Woman sighed.

She touched the little red hand with her finger and the fist immediately opened and closed around it.

Her finger was the aged gray of bark in the circlet of minute coral fingers.

"Perhaps you can leave them here for a few days," she said slowly, "until your people see that they bring no harm to anyone. Then...."

"Thank you, Spider Grandmother."

The young woman began to climb very rapidly up the ladder toward the roof.

"Only for a little while," Spider Woman called after her.

But even as the words floated up with the gossamer smoke, she knew the young woman would never be back.

KOKOPELLI

When the people emerged from the sipapu,
they were accompanied by Kokopelli,
the Humped Back Flute Player,
who was renowned for his lovemaking.
—OLD PUEBLO MYTH

HE had a slight curve in his spine, but it somehow only made him more attractive, more indomitable with the almost unnoticeable limp that he disguised as he raced the young men of their pueblo and almost always carried off the bow trophy of the races. That faintest of arches in his back seemed to make him hunt and go without water longer than the others, seek harder, range farther, and he was the one who most often ran the deer to breathlessness, held the foaming nostrils against the sand until the air and the life were gone. And thus it was that he was also the most sought after young man in the pueblo, the one to whom the marriageable girls of the village brought their fresh corn balls, the one whom they constantly saluted on their walks beside the adobe houses, the one whom they invited first into the ring at the dances.

But when he came to her mother's house after the long dance and said, "I want to marry your daughter," she was without words, for she had never dared dream of herself with him.

And when she answered nothing, but only stared at his great and manly beauty, her mother said, "Do you wish to marry this young man?"

She nodded, still unable to say anything, and he smiled with his eyes like flakes of obsidian.

"Then you may go into the other room together," her mother said. "In the morning I shall go to the bow priests and announce the betrothal."

She could only nod silently. He took her hand and led her beneath the blanket that was hung between the two rooms. She knew her hand was very cold in his.

"Make us a fire," he said when they were in the room. He sat down on her blanket, and she nodded again.

How had he possibly chosen her of all their village girls who wanted to marry him? She had never dreamed of herself, even in her most rainbowed imaginings, as his bride. Always the other pueblo girls had surrounded him, and she'd had only glimpses of him in the square, at the races or the dances. How had the kachinas given her such good fortune?

The little flame leaped from the circle of stones and she could see his eyes like black coals alight. "Why did you choose me for your wife?" she said across the tiny fire. "We have rarely spoken in all the days you have been in our village."

He motioned for her to come to him.

"You are different from the rest," he said softly as he pulled her down beside him onto the blanket and held her with arms the shade of polished hickory in the firelight. "You have a strength that I want in a woman, in my wife."

She looked into his face.

His arms tightened. "You stand aloof from the others," he said. "And you are strong in your aloneness."

He released her momentarily, unfastened the sash and the blanket dress that fell back from her breasts and hips, and his black eyes watched her body as he removed his necklaces, bracelets, his own fringed buckskins. Then he pressed her to his warm chest, lay her back on the blanket, and spread her thighs with his.

The fire had not yet died as she awoke and looked at his sleeping body beside her, the delicate bend of his vertebrae that was both his flaw and his distinction, and she wanted to kiss the gentle curve of his back that she had loved ever since he appeared from the south, arriving at their pueblo with his great packet of seed corn he had brought to trade for turquoise.

But she didn't stir or wake him, and she lay watching his beautiful form. How could she have been the one of all their pueblo to have ensnared such a handsome traveler?

She was still awake when he opened his eyes and smiled at her again. He reached out and touched her loosened hair, stroked down her neck to her breast and her flat stomach.

"Are you happy, my wife?"

Her throat was too closed with happiness for words as he caressed her hip, buttock, parted her thighs once more, and held her hard as he entered her again.

When she awoke once more he was gone, and she dressed slowly, carefully, braiding sacred turkey feathers in her hair for the ceremony.

She was conscious of the hot and jealous stares of the other girls as she came up to their roof and descended the ladder into the ritual of the wedding, but she watched only his shining black eyes, his glowing face as they became man and wife.

She avoided the other girls in the early weeks of her happiness as his wife, knowing their envy, preferring her own silent roof, grinding her corn alone for his meal. And the days passed with counted noons, with wordless nights beside the blanket-sheltered fires.

She continued to marvel at her luck as she watched his smile, his eyes on her, as he disappeared below the roof each morning, as she watched him prepare his bow for the hunt, his hoe for the field. The moon had vanished, had reappeared to thicken into a white shell disc three times before she noticed other things beyond her roof, before at last she forced herself to hear the other voices.

"These many days he has been bedding Loping Antelope's wife," her mother said, not glancing up from her endlessly circling mano. The roof air was silent but for the sound of pitted stones against the crushing grains of corn.

She brushed the powdered meal into a wedding basket. Through the mist that had suddenly clouded her sight, she saw that the sun was almost in the center of the sky.

"You have been in other women's beds," she said to him that evening when he had finished the deer strips and the corn balls and was resting on his bench, satisfied with her careful food.

He looked at her. "But you are my wife."

"In our village a husband and a wife are one. If they do not want to be together as one, they take their separate paths."

He beckoned her to join him on the bench, but she stayed immobile on her blanket by the fire. He leaned forward, his elbows on his knees. "You love me and you want me."

She hesitated. Then she said, "I am strong enough to live without you."

His eyes were a pupilless black upon her. "You love me because of my prowess. You wouldn't want a husband who was not the best at hunting, the best in bed. You wouldn't want a husband who could not satisfy many women."

She watched him from across the flickering evening fire, and she knew that he didn't understand, that he couldn't understand.

"It is time for you to go to another village," she said.

He started to speak, but she stood up and shook her head with pity as she looked down on him and saw from that angle the very discernible hump in his back.

THE FLOOD

The people had not found the exact Center.
The earth rumbled
and the water spouted through the sipapu.
The people fled to Corn Mountain
away from the flood.
—ANCIENT ZUÑI MYTH

SHE gazed across the room at them, their little heads bent over the corn husk dolls in their laps, and she wanted to stroke the sleek hair, the firm round cheeks. But she knew that hugging them only embarrassed them. She'd raised them to be independent, to be self-sufficient, even to be able to fix their own corn balls in the heated water basket if she were in the field, and she knew that she had to restrain her impulses to fling her arms around them both and squeeze them like the dolls they seemed.

They'd never know what it was costing her to control herself, to keep from fondling them every time they were in her sight.

They'd never know what it was costing her to marry their uncle, their dead father's brother, who was no more like their handsome father than a scrub oak was like a pinon pine.

But what else could she do? How could they live if no one were there to bring the deer?

21

She glanced down quickly as her eyes filled with involuntary tears. It wouldn't do for them to see her crying.

She rubbed hard at the corn on her metate which she couldn't see around the salt film.

To have to take to bed one whose very flesh was repugnant to her touch.

She should be grateful for his offer, the unmarried elder brother, who had stayed with their mother when his younger brother had married, gone off to his wife's clan, but somehow she couldn't be. It was as if he belonged to their mother, the old woman with the clutching hands, as if he were the old woman's husband rather than her son, and she had no desire to be a second wife.

The tears overflowed her lower lids, splashed on the back of her hand that circled the stone mano over the speckled corn.

If there were only some other way.

But she'd thought too long as it was, delayed as long as she'd dared, until her brother-in-law was becoming impatient, or at least his mother was, sensing some offense to her son, and even then, he might take back his offer of marriage.

She dared not sniff back the tears and alert them that something was wrong. She had to keep their world intact, had to act as if all were well and natural in their sheltered yet self-sufficient sphere. She glanced up at them through her lashes.

But they were still engrossed in their play, the dolls they had equipped with miniature bows and arrows and were about to send into a miniature war.

She loved to watch them when they weren't aware of her eyes. They were so alert, so assured for their years, and almost everyone in the pueblo had commented at one time or another on how well they were accepting their father's untimely death.

They never knew what that had meant to her either, that accidental death; they would never know how the terrible controlled mourning had locked her heart in mortar of stone. Sometimes she'd felt that she couldn't live with the pain in her chest, but as she'd stared through the roof square into the infinite stars through the infinite cold nights, she knew she had to live for them. She had to rise the next morning, and the one after that, had to boil a usual cornmeal breakfast and grind a basket of unaltering corn.

She took a deep breath that she tried to disguise as a half lazy yawn so they wouldn't notice anything amiss.

But just at that moment, the adobe floor swayed slightly and a rumbling occurred somewhere far off.

"What was that, Momma?"

But they were touching the floor with their little hands, steadying themselves, staring up at the roof hole with curiosity rather than fright.

"A small earthquake. They happen sometimes in the hot summer," she said calmly, even as her blood beat faster in her wrists.

"Oh." They nodded.

Then the floor churned under them again. The children braced themselves but still toppled into each other.

"Oh!"

But she saw that they were grinning as they fell over onto the cracking, buckling, adobe of the floor.

"Come out quickly!" A yell came from the roof, and she recognized her brother-in-law's call despite the quavering of the voice. "Come quickly!" His face peered into the square. "Everyone is fleeing. Come! Hurry!"

The floor paused in its rocking, but she could feel that the tremor was not over. When it started again, the adobe bricks of the house and roof would fall in upon them.

"Up you go. Your uncle has come to take us to safety." She couldn't yet bear to refer to him as their future father, but she told herself to remember the measure of gratitude he deserved for his coming. "Up the ladder with you both," she added, swatting them each lightly as they started up, letting them know by her touch that it was merely a lark of some sort.

The ground was heaving again by the time she reached the open square onto the roof, and she was barely able to hold the rungs.

The sun was shining brightly and the incongruous emptiness of the calm sky belied the lurching of the earth.

"Hurry!" He was shouting even though she was now nearby. "Water has begun flowing up through the sipapu in the kiva, up through many of the cook pits of the houses."

"What is it?"

He helped her up onto the roof and her bare arm could feel the calluses of his palm.

"The bow priests say that the earth is angry. That we haven't found the Center and are raising our children to be without compassion."

His eyes were more frightened than the children's.

"Look, Momma."

They were at the edge of the roof, clinging to each other, staring down into the street.

"The people have almost all fled to Corn Mountain. I must go carry my aged mother to safety," he said loudly close to her ear. "Go to Corn Mountain as quickly as you can."

Before she could do more than nod, he was over the edge of the roof and down the ladder.

"Come, children, we're going to Corn Mountain." She could no longer make it sound like an outing, but she kept her tone as calm and neutral as possible as she lifted one and then the other onto the ladder.

When she reached the ladder herself she could hear the water bubbling, gurgling up from the storage pit inside their own house.

She swung down from the last rung just as the earth shook itself again, and she lost her balance, her leg turning under her as she fell, twisting at the firm lacings of her boot.

"Ah-h-h!"

She heard the bone crack and she fell over on her elbow.

"Look!" the children said and pointed.

A stream was beginning to flow down the street, a gentle stream of crystal water that swayed with the earth.

She tried to get up, but the twist of her leg wouldn't straighten. The pain shot agonizingly up her thigh.

"I can't go," she said softly, but they were too far away to hear her. She leaned back against the wall and watched the street that had become a widened stream.

The children ran over to her again. "Look at the water!" they said excitedly. "It's like a river running right through the village."

One of them jostled her shoulder and pointed.

"Yes, dear." She took a deep breath. "But you can't stay to watch it turn into a pool. Pretty soon it will be too deep for you to walk in."

They were staring at it fascinated as it swirled around the corner of a house and lapped over their feet. It covered her knee, the leg whose snapped bone was pressing the flesh from within, trying to burst through.

"You must go up that way to higher ground until you reach Corn Mountain and the rest of our people," she said, taking each one by the hand and pointing with her head toward the hill beyond their village.

"Aren't you coming with us?"

She forced her hands on theirs not to grip, not to hold too tightly.

"Not right now, but you must hurry along before the water gets too high for you."

She let go of their hands and gave them light playful pushes to get them started. "Why not run and see who can win by getting to the path up the hill first?"

Another surge of the water swayed higher, reached her waist.

"Ready, set, go!"

And they ran, splashing in the water up to their knees, their little legs churning it, spraying it delightedly.

The sun gazed down hot and drying as the water surged higher, swirled, and rose.

It was at her shoulders when she saw them around the corner of the street, saw them gain the hill and start up the path.

It was no longer a stream or a tiny river, but a lake now, each of whose swelling waves lapped a little higher on the walls.

She craned her neck, lifting herself with her palms against the wall to keep the water from her nostrils a second longer.

She had made them so strong, so secure that they would be all right.

There they were, free of the water, heading up the slope from the village, going toward Corn Mountain.

She wanted to scream out their names, raise an arm that they could see her one last time and remember. But they were facing the top of the hill, and neither of them was looking back.

COYOTE'S WAGER

In the very beginning of the world,
the Coyote was more foolish than he is now;
then he was the most ignorant of all the animals.
— YAQUI LEGEND

He has desired you for a long time."

"Has he?" She hacked at the smoothed stone metate with a pounding rock to roughen the surface.

"Haven't you seen him at the dances watching you when he thought no one was close?"

"Hm-m-m-m." She probably had felt his eyes on her in the liquid movements of the kiva dances without being aware of it.

Coyote leaned against the adobe wall. "That was why he was willing to wager three blankets," he smiled, "and that fine flint knife of his."

"Three blankets?" They had only another blanket in addition to the one she wore, and no flint knives at all.

"Against one night with you."

She glanced up quickly from her work on the metate.

He laughed. "Don't be startled. There's no way he can win. It's a bet for innocents. He can dig all right, with the best of them, but nobody in the pueblo is as swift as I am." He tapped his sleek brown thigh. "These are runner's legs. The wager is only for the first four rabbits. And then we'll have all the blankets we need, and I'll own that beautiful flint knife with the turquoise handle."

She looked at him for a second without speaking and then began hammering again on the metate.

He got up and patted her bare shoulder as he went by. "Don't give it any other thought. Badger can never bring back four rabbits before I do."

He went up the ladder.

She glanced up into the night sky jabbed thick with stars like kachina eyes.

She hadn't thought of being with another man besides her husband. Another man's body. Another man's arms and breath.

She realized the surface of the metate had been pocked with more than enough gouges to crack the corn kernels and she quit pounding.

Footsteps touched the roof and the ladder poles shivered as someone balanced above on the top rung.

She hadn't expected him back so soon. She looked up.

But it was Badger Man instead.

He came easily down the ladder and stepped off, looking long at her.

"You have heard of the wager?"

She nodded.

He knelt down, squatted on his heels to look straight into her face. "I know a rabbit barrow very near the village that houses a dozen rabbits. Coyote was so sure of his swift racing ability that he was willing to bet anything, even something that is most precious to him." His eyes were very dark and they stared unwaveringly into hers. "But the barrow I know of is so close, that skill in running counts for nothing. Only digging is important."

She didn't say anything. She'd never seen him that close before, never noticed how smooth and gleaming his hair was.

"This you may tell him if you do not want me to win the wager."

He wore a double strand of turquoise beads around his neck. She'd never seen such rich green turquoise, polished like oiled leaves.

"I never interfere with my husband's wagers." Even when he bet and lost her beautiful funeral bowls with the diamond rabbit centers. "I will leave the outcome to the kachinas who rule such things. Perhaps your barrow will be empty when you go at dawn. Perhaps my husband will stumble across a nest of rabbits outside our wall."

He gazed at her with his dark, dark stare. "Perhaps."

Then he stood up and went back up the ladder.

And when Coyote returned home, she said nothing of the visit.

But that night she couldn't sleep and stared into the sky hole until the night stars paled against the color of ashes and disappeared.

In the dawn light, Coyote rose, greased himself for the race, braided his hair that the wind wouldn't catch in it and slow him.

"Don't worry," he said as he took four prayer sticks from the eaves. "I'll return with the rabbits long before Badger Man is even awake."

When he had gone, she folded the blanket, dressed, and plaited her own black hair with sacred turkey feathers. She didn't know why she had felt the need for the turkey feathers, and she said no words of prayer as she twisted them into her braids, but somehow she wanted the delicate eider touch, the slender quills, against her neck.

And instead of the white corn she'd intended to grind, she took out her small olla of precious sweet corn. She would prepare sweet cakes for the evening meal.

She carried the metate, the mano, and the woven trays to the roof. In the white blue of the morning she ground the kernels into soft dust, glanced occasionally at the heat shimmers beyond the mesa. She purposely thought of nothing as she worked, and she was on the final grinding when her husband came up to the roof.

Hairs straggled loose from his morning braids, sweat had streaked through the oil on his body.

"It was not a fair contest," he said at last. "But the bow priests have declared that it stands."

She didn't say anything.

"It will be for this one night only." He looked out over the desert that was staining mauve with the sunset. "I will spend the night in the kiva. Badger is gentle. It is only for one night."

She nodded without answering and he went away.

While the clouds empurpled the rim of the mountains, she finished the grinding and carried the fine corn flour down into the house. She made the sweet corn cakes and baked them in the fire.

Badger came down the ladder without a word.

"I have prepared food," she said.

He nodded, spread the blanket he had brought, and sat down crosslegged on it as he gazed at her. "The race went as I said."

She served the cakes and sat down with him on the blanket. It was soft and thick. "Eat."

He took one of the cakes as he watched her. The fire glowed on his turquoise necklaces.

"My husband says you are gentle as he is."

He lifted the basket of corn cakes from her hand and put it carefully aside. Then he unfastened the sash of the blanket she wore and pulled her to him.

He was not gentle.

"I have desired you longer than I can remember," he said above her as he made love fiercely, angrily. "But you were not my wife."

He led her with clenched teeth, led her body into arched shuddering before him. They lay back spent together on the thick blanket. He held her close against his side, entwined his legs with hers as they slept.

Sometime in the night before the stars had faded, he awoke and made fierce love to her again. "I shall have no other wife but you," he said.

She nodded against his shoulder, feeling the hard knotted tenseness of his arms.

They slept once more, but he kept his arms tight around her.

The sunlight was already spilling through the square in the roof when she opened her eyes. He was watching her.

"Have you regrets?"

She shook her head.

"Then I shall go to the bow priests to proclaim our bethrothal in the kiva."

She nodded. "Coyote's moccasins will be outside when he returns and he will know before he hears the announcement."

He reached for one of the strands of turquoise that he had tossed aside in the night and put it over her head. He lifted the uncoiled mass of her hair to settle the beads around her neck. "Until our marriage," he said.

Then he dressed and went out, pausing to look down at her from the top of the ladder.

They smiled.

After she had braided her hair once more, she found a pair of moccasins, old and stiff, poorly stitched from hide that had once been soaked and had curled in wooden twists back upon itself.

She carried them outside and dropped them down off the roof.

They thudded into the dirt, ugly and poor, the sun's beaten silver eye exposing them unremittingly. She debated about tossing something else down with them, a stone maul, a handful of turkey feathers.

Poor gentle Coyote who didn't know so many things.

She looked briefly at the cracked and hardened leather of the shoes and went back inside.

ATOCLE WOMAN

Their grandmother, Spider Woman, had warned them
to stay away from Atocle Woman who lived nearby.
But the Little War Twins decided
to go see the evil woman anyway.
—ANCIENT ZUÑI MYTH

SHE'D seen them from far away,
ranging mountains other than hers, leaping rainbows, racing
dawns, true children of the sun, those twin grandsons of old Spider
Woman, but she'd never seen them as near as they were at that moment, climbing toward her cave.

They were indeed handsome, possibly the handsomest young
men she'd ever seen, dressed in shimmering buckskins pale as morning, buckskins she could tell even from that distance would be as
soft as the petals of a primrose.

She watched them climb, slip on the sheered glass of the obsidian,
chip yet another foothold, and try again. Hers was the only cave on
the black mountain, and she knew they had to be coming to see her.

She went back inside to set out strips of dried deer meat and some
of her prized blue-black parched corn for them. She glanced at the
black opal stalagmites, the stalactites of moist black pearl looped
beneath her ceiling, and she knew that her jeweled cave would surprise and please them.

It had been long since any man had come from the pueblo. She was aware of what they said about her in the mesa village, but it had never mattered. What could such ignorant people really know? And she was used to being by herself, alone with the rains and mists of the black mountain.

But now the handsome grandsons of old Spider Woman were paying her a visit, and she felt her wrists, her throat blood beat faster. They were coming, dressed in their coral necklaces, milkshell bracelets, each carrying a fine ceremonial atlatl of polished turquoise.

She went outside, once more pausing in the dark shade rim to await their arrival.

And when their sandals were loud upon the rain-washed onyx pebbles and she at last saw the head, the broad muscled shoulders of the twin in the lead, her breath quickened to the beat of her temples.

"We have come," the young man said as his creamy buckskinned thighs, knees, his narrow sandaled feet climbed into view and his brother appeared behind him.

"You are welcome," she said ritualistically, glancing away from their eyes. Her face felt as if she'd been hours in the white sun.

"I have food," she added and motioned them into the cave out of the baked noon heat.

They ducked into the entrance and when she followed them, she saw in the glow of the hematite crystals that they were even more handsome than she'd thought.

They sat down and looked at her cave, their eyes wide with child awe.

"Eat," she said and placed the fine pitch-caulked baskets of meat and ebony corn before them.

How strong and young they were, how exactly alike.

"Our grandmother didn't want us to come," one of them said, gazing around as he chewed a strip of the deer meat. "But Elder Brother had heard much about you and wanted to come."

The other twin smiled at her, and something in her chest lurched, twisted against the inner lining of her ribs.

"Younger Brother didn't want to be left at home, so he came also," he said and put the kernels of corn in his mouth one at a time, cracking them between his beautiful strong white teeth.

The glittering black crystals around them threw shadows on their thin noses, their marble foreheads.

"Your grandmother has never been one of my friends," she said carefully.

Elder Brother shrugged. "It doesn't matter what my grandmother thinks." He looked at her steadily with his smile. "I make up my own mind."

And the thudding in her throat hollow grew in volume, pounding at her neck bones.

"I have no daughter," she said softly, sensing but afraid to believe what she was sure she saw in his smile.

"I know," he said as he reached out his hand and laid it on her arm.

His fingers were as strong, as cool as silver.

She couldn't remember when a man had touched her last. Once there were many men who came, and one in particular with sparkling obsidian eyes and a strength in his arms of living granite. He had come to her cave with deer and rabbits, an atlatl of iron wood, a necklace of jasper beads. They had lain together in her glittering cave, had sat, hands touching, through many darkenings of the moon. But then Spider Woman had told him things about her and he had not come again. Neither he nor the others, and now....

"They tell many stories of me in the pueblo, but the tales have little truth in them."

They both nodded, and Elder Brother's firm cool hand came up to touch her chin, the side of her face. "The old people of the pueblo, my grandmother among them, have forgotten what the truth is," he said.

She realized that she was holding her breath.

They ate, and she watched them without meeting their eyes, keeping herself motionless as stone.

Then as the deer meat and the corn were low in the black rimmed baskets, Elder Brother said, "Have you another room, Atocle Woman?" and his hand moved down to her shoulder.

She nodded, and he reached down, helped her rise from the sable blanket. He stood brushing against her lightly, his chest beside her arm. He was much taller than she was, very young and straight.

"You wait here, Younger Brother," he said.

And she led the way through the shining jet icicles, into the back vault of the cave.

"I am glad I came," he said close behind her, and his whisper echoed, ached in her wrists.

"You must stoop here," she said, glancing back at him. "You are very tall."

Taller than any man who had ever been in the inner room of her cave.

He smiled and took her hand as they went together into the smaller alcove, letting the raven blanket drop down over the circular stone doorway.

Then he stopped, stood and looked around at the niches hollowed in the gleaming black stone. His fingers let go of hers.

"Is this where you keep the sacred rain-making bow?" he asked in a voice that attempted to be offhand.

And she knew.

He hadn't come for her at all.

"Is this it?" He was on the far side of the cave room, the bow, the sacred lightning arrow in his metal cold hand. "It is, isn't it?"

He had the sky blue atlatl in his other hand, and she hadn't noticed until then that he'd carried it with him, the polished stone slick, greased in his palm. Nor had she noticed the snow-fur quiver until he reached behind him, and without loosing the rain bow and the lighting arrow, extracted a spear of hard white pine, fitted it to the atlatl and pointed it at her.

"My grandmother said that you were very pretty in your day, that your night beauty took many men away from the fair women of our pueblo. She said that even my grandfather once...."

But she wasn't listening as she watched him pull back his pallid arm, flick the atlatl and the slivered ashen dart. She saw it leave the daylight stone and felt the rain begin to weep down in mist from the walls, begin to pelt the darkened cave.

BAHOLIKONGA

The people were living at Yellow Village.
The sacred spring of Baholikonga was nearby.
—OLD HOPI MYTH

VARIANT #1

SHE watched him from behind the screen of willows, watched the sun on his smooth firm muscles, on his wet flesh as he swam nude in the pool far below her. He dove and the center of the water sucked inward, closed over where he had been as the waves expanded in widening circles until they collapsed onto the outer stones and became the lapping edge of the pool.

She waited, staring intently without breathing as another concentric set of the liquid circles spread outward, waited until at last he broke from the surface once more and shook the clinging drops from his face. The tiny crystal spheres sprayed in miniature suns from his eyebrows and chin and she felt her stomach twist with desire as she held herself rigid in her green branched cover.

His bronzed body in the water was so beautiful.

And she watched as he swam, watched with eyes that didn't swerve from the pool until the sun began to slant across the mesas

35

and roast them a deep evening purple, until the shadows sur-
rounding her had thickened to jade and she could sense the night
coolness lacing her emerald shade. Then she carefully, soundlessly,
even though she knew she was too far from where he still splashed
in the water to hear her movements, slipped on her sandals and
backed away from the narrow forest that grew beside the pool.

She stopped to retrieve the basket of cattails she'd thought to pull
before she came to the gallery forest, the basket of green fruits and
sharp leaves that were the excuse for her daily avoidance of the
village.

He swam there every afternoon, and she knew she wouldn't be
able to resist returning the next day and the next to observe him
secretly.

But she also knew that it would remain a secret vigil, that she
would never reveal her adoration. Or even her presence there in the
hillock of willows above the rock-lined pool. For she was plain.
Without plumpness or full thighs or breasts, she was possibly the
plainest girl in their village, destined to be some grateful second
wife, taken into another woman's pueblo for expediency or for the
blankets her father would willingly contribute to the other woman's
household.

The tendons of her throat ached with the words of love that she
could never speak to him, and, as she walked, her head burned with
images of him, beautiful, flashing, diving in the blue reflecting disc
of water.

The sky had washed gray with twilight as she reached the village.
Her mother was waiting on the roof, watching her approach with
anxious but suspicious eyes. Yet all her mother said was, "I see you
brought more rushes for baskets."

She nodded. "I have many designs for new baskets in my head."

And she went down into the room where the fire flared and the
corn balls boiled for the evening meal. She peeled the cattails, laid
them in neat green rows to eat with the corn. When her father came
in from the roof doorway, she found many questions to ask about
the planting dances and evaded her mother's stare.

But as the evening meal and the dusk were finished, and she went
into the inner room to roll herself in her blanket, she heard her
mother's voice. "Something is wrong. Our daughter is distracted,

and I have come upon her many times of late with the gaze that appears only with a first falling in love. She vanishes from the pueblo every afternoon, and I think...."

She listened closely, but she couldn't hear her father's words, and after a pause her mother added, "I too have those same fears. Perhaps she is meeting a young man not of our people, perhaps even an Apache."

Her blood thudded, pressed swollen against her skull, nearly bursting through the thin flesh of her temples, and she lay still in the blackness of the room.

But she couldn't sleep, and in the dawn she left the house before her parents were awake, crept from the pueblo before the yellow light began to seep into the corn fields.

She'd neglected to bring a basket or even a water jug in her haste, and in her hurry she was careless as she approached the willows, the turquoise deep of the pool. She blundered too quickly, stumbling upon the ring of water from an unsheltered side.

He was already there in the morning stillness, and she knew that he'd observed her before she could draw back into the shadow of the trees.

"Wait!" he called. "I've seen you here in the afternoons. Don't go!"

"I must...," she began, shrinking against the nearest willow trunk. "You have seen me?"

"Yes." He was at the edge of the pool, but he made no move to climb out of the water. "There in the trees." And he nodded toward the rise, toward the dense center of the forest where she'd sat and felt herself protected those many afternoons. "I thought at first you might be bringing prayersticks or sacred meal to the pool. But you never came down," he added when she didn't say anything.

"I...." But she couldn't meet his eyes or continue. She could feel the blood suffuse her cheeks, betray her confusion. She'd never envisioned herself talking to him.

She heard him float slightly away from the border stones, tread water, and then swim back near the edge again. She stared down at the black rocks, gleaming with the shimmering polish of wetness.

"I am not for you," he said gently.

"Oh, no. Of course not," she blurted quickly. "I had no illusions of...." How obvious she must have been, even in the forest, as transparent as the crystal water even in the green webbing of the trees, that he could have discerned her hopeless love so easily. "I am much too plain to ever...."

"No!" he said, his voice almost thundering, amplified by the water.

Startled, she glanced into his face. He was staring at her and there was something in his eyes that she couldn't understand.

"No," he added in a softer tone. "That's not what I meant." He seemed to be studying her features with curiosity. "Whoever told you that you were plain?"

"Why, in the entire pueblo, there is not one young man who would ever...."

He was shaking his head. "How blind they must be, those eyeless young men of your pueblo."

The rush of her blood that had almost subsided surged again, and her gaze reddened once more. But she kept watching his eyes.

And a silence spread in slow circles as the yellow light dropped from the horizon, stained the desert sand. Then at last he said in such a low voice that she wasn't sure he was speaking aloud even though she saw his lips move, "I only meant that I am immortal, that I live beneath the waters."

"Yes, I know."

"But your presence here beside the sacred pool has made my loneliness a little easier to bear."

And she recognized the pain in his eyes.

"I too have been lonely," she said.

He didn't answer, merely shook his head again as he sank into the water, his eyes recording, devouring her as he disappeared slowly into the blue depths.

She knelt beside the stones, stared into the sacred lake as the sun lifted into the middle of the sky and dried it white bone hot. But she didn't move into the cooler shadows of the trees. Nor did she stir when the blazing reflection of the sun eased down again, fell into the mountain rim.

If she went back to the pueblo, they might forbid her returning to the pool, they might refuse her pleas, forbid her very breath and life.

And she waited on her heels, hugged her skirt around her knees while the darkness came and the sheered disc of the moon sought its broken other half in the motionless black pool.

The star points hung suspended, sharp and clear, but she didn't notice them. Nor did she see the cold stars pale, recede, and the sky lighten once more. She remained immobile on the pebbled bank, waiting, watching only for the first parting of the water.

Finally, a minute fountain bubbled, then the glittering mica smoothness whipped to foam, and his head at last emerged from the whirling spring.

"You have come again," he said quietly.

She nodded, reached out and carefully touched his gentle face, brushed back the sodden plume that drooped from the bronze horn on his forehead.

Then she leaned down and removed her sandals, stepped over the rim of the stones, waded to her knees toward him.

His muscles tensed as he coiled near her.

"As much as I want you to come with me," he said, "I must warn you that you may drown."

She put her arms around the sleek cool serpent body, placed her cheek on his, pressed herself tight against him as they began to submerge in the sacred water together. "I know," she said.

VARIANT #2

WHAT can we tell your father or the bow priest or the rest of the village once you begin to show?" her mother moaned in a voice like rustling yucca. "They will never accept a man of our own clan as the father."

She slid the mano along the pecked stone, watched the corn grains tumble into powder. "I have already thought about it. I plan to tell them that while I was bathing in the sacred spring, I became

pregnant by the Horned Water Serpent," she said calmly. She pressed
the cracked corn hard between the stones, seeing, but not glancing up
at her mother's forlorn gestures. "No one will dare contradict me."

"How can you be so sure? What if someone has seen you with
Crow Wing and...."

She shrugged, irritated by her mother's panic. "No one has seen
us together, and not one of our people has ever seen the Water Serpent. Who is there to dispute that my child is that of Baholikonga?"

"Yes, but what if...."

"That's enough." She raised her voice, scowled with disgust at the
timid woman on the roof beside her, then lowered her voice again.
"I have decided. I will say that the pregnancy came from my accidental immersion in the hallowed water, that the newborn will be
part kachina, part divine, a shaman for our clan." She sifted the
corn, stirred it with her finger. "After the birth, Crow Wing and I
can raise the child as brother and sister."

Her mother continued to twist her hands despairingly across her
stomach, but at last she looked away in silence.

And when the bow priest came with her father for the evening
meal, her mother remained silent upon her declaration that
Baholikonga had empowered her with his seed, that in six months
she would present their clan with a demigod.

"Is this true, my daughter?" the bow priest asked, searching her
face with his keen black eyes.

"Yes, grandfather." She was certain he had no suspicion of his
own nephew. Her glance never wavered.

The bow priest stared at her and the fire sent colorless smoke
toward the square hole in the roof. Finally he nodded. "It is a great
privilege for our clan," he said at last.

"Yes, grandfather."

"We will honor this child with ritual ceremonies and many
prayersticks as your time comes close, my daughter."

"Thank you, grandfather."

He thoughtfully bit into a cornball. "You must go at dawn to the
sacred well to give thanks to the Horned Water Serpent for so great
a gift. Take this prayer meal ground with turquoise." He drew a
softened deerskin pouch from his belt and held it out to her.

"Thank you, grandfather," she said again, glanced toward her mother in her corner, then let her eyelids drop demurely.

And the next morning at dawn she tucked the little deerskin bag, as delicate as sheltered moss, into her sash and strode from the village.

When she reached the narrow forest that grew beside the sacred spring, she paused to loosen the drawstring of the little bag and emptied the blessed meal into her hand.

In the ashen morning light, the crushed grains of many-colored corn, the azure chips of turquoise sparkled, bejeweled, and she gazed down at them pleased by their rainbow hues, by her own cleverness, by the ease with which she'd won the old bow priest's approval. When the baby had been born, it would be simple enough to convince the old man that she and Crow Wing should be together.

She almost lifted up her palm to tip the multi-colored fragments to her tongue, but then she didn't, and merely smiled, began to trail the bits of corn and ground turquoise along the sand at the edge of the pool.

Suddenly the water surged, frothed, erupted around the glittering head of the Horned Water Serpent.

She started, and the meal sprayed from her fingers, dusted her own ankles, sandals.

He rose high out of the pool, held her captive with his endless reptilian eyes, strangely dry in his face that streamed with water.

"I understand that you have said you are with child by me, Baholikonga," he boomed in a voice that crashed over her, echoed into the trees.

She stared at him in mute horror.

"I have heard the rumor and I have come to take you with me as my bride," he said when no sound issued from her opened mouth.

"But I...."

"I wish to raise the child myself," he added fiercely, and his body broke from the water, coiled harshly around her before she could flee.

His muscles were as cold as hammered metal, icily hard around her.

She found her voice as he pulled her, lifted her rapidly over the side of the pool. "You know the child is not yours!"

"But after I take you as my wife, your people will never doubt your word. They will believe with certainty that your pregnancy was indeed sacred," he said calmly without loosening his hold.

"You are an immortal and I am not!" she cried as the icy water swirled, sucked at her knees.

Her arms and hands were clamped to her sides by his wet plated coils.

He nodded.

The water reached her sash, the undersides of her breasts.

They began to submerge together, and her stricken eyes fastened on the scarlet feather, the still damp plume attached to the burnished horn of his forehead. "But I could drown," she shouted and tried to lift her chin above the freezing water.

He coiled tighter, more rigidly around her. "I know," he said.

SALT WOMAN

The people were careless and misused the supply of salt.
The Salt Mother was very sad and went away.
And when the people came to where
the salt lake had been, there was no lake.
—ANCIENT ZUÑI MYTH

IT pleased her that they came to her, the entire pueblo, came to her tiny alkali lake, weekly, sometimes daily if they had much meat to preserve. They were always so polite as she ladled the white salt into their fine woven baskets or their carefully painted bowls. She noticed that they never brought blackened cookware or everyday baskets to carry away her salt the way she'd heard they did with Pine Maiden's piñon nuts when they went up into the hills. They knew the value of her salt and they watched her with seed dark eyes each time they had given her their cut drilled shells in exchange for her handful of salt. The disc shell beads were almost as white as her salt but not quite, and while she threaded them on twisted fique strings into necklaces for her husband, she always wished the shells had been just a little snowier, just a little more glistening, that he would ever be reminded she had traded her salt to get him necklaces, many valuable necklaces that lay upon his strong wide chest and reflected in coiled strands the whiteness of his teeth.

43

He was strong, so tall and straight, and she was glad to be able to get the necklaces and the occasional carved shell bracelets for his muscled forearm that was the color of sleek tanned hide. She needed nothing for herself in return for her salt. She knew she wasn't beautiful, and while she had learned to paint her cheekbones, her forehead, with designs that made her appear almost beautiful, she knew that the necklaces on her flat chest would have added nothing to their, or to her, beauty.

They should be for him.

She accepted a final offering of smoothed, near-white beads and stood immobile, solemn, as the last suppliant (she never thought of them as buyers) bowed to her.

"Thank you, grandmother."

They were always so polite.

The man's black eyes looked at her as if he would add another word as he secured the salt in his basket, but then he backed away a few steps, turned, and started up the winding path to the mesa pueblo.

She watched him, an old man with a twisted foot, go up toward the village, and then she went down the ladder into the house that was their place to be alone. She took the white blanket and spread it carefully for her husband's coming, stirred the tiny fire beneath its ring of stones so that the pot of water could heat and boil the corn balls fresh and hot for his noon meal.

The little flames made yellow and black shadows on the roof poles, sent yellow streaks across the salt that mounded like new snow in the corner of the room. Pure, clean white salt, flesh of her flesh, glittering like a new blown drift in the winter sun.

She looked at the slope of the precious salt and judged it. There would be enough to get him a bracelet inlaid with turquoise.

"Salt Woman, I have come." The greeting fell from the blue roof opening in a woman's voice and surprised her. She had not heard anyone above her on the roof.

"Enter."

She watched the beautiful young woman climb down the ladder. A young woman in fine clothes, a soft black blanket and a delicate fringed sash. Her full breasts were draped with many shell necklaces, and row upon row of glycimeris bracelets clacked upon her plump arms.

"How have you lived these days?" the young woman asked in ceremonial greeting.

"Happily, thank you." She bowed, gestured toward the meal that waited to be boiled. "You are welcome to my house. I shall prepare food."

"No." The young woman held up her hand to stay the preparations. "No. I have come only to tell you that I love your husband." The round eyes gazed from an unlined, unpainted face. "And he loves me." The smooth dimpled hand touched the necklace strands. "He has given me many presents to show his love. But he will not leave you because he says that you need him."

She saw then the lengths of beads that she herself had strung, the white drilled shells almost as white as her own salt, and she knew that what the young woman said was true.

"He is such a wonderful man," the young plump voice continued, the young round eyes reflecting flames from the tiny stone-ringed fire. "We love each other very much."

And she was sure that that too was true.

"I thought if you knew, Salt Woman, you would let him go."

She should have known that he was too young and strong to stay with her, that he....

"Yes," she said to the glowing, unpainted face. "I will let him go."

The lips that were the luscious purple of ripe cactus pears smiled slightly. "You are a good and wise woman."

They must all have known, each of the villagers, coming with their palmful of beads, all known of her husband with the young woman to whom he gave the necklaces. All of them looking at her with their charcoal eyes. How foolish she must have seemed, stringing beads one by one that went to enfold the plump young neck of a....

She gazed stonily into the fire and did not watch the young woman climb back up the ladder, did not respond to the ritual farewell.

She would of course go away.

Far from the pueblo. Into the north where they would not know of her shame, or her foolishness.

She rose, stepped to the edge of the little hill of salt, the grains like dry white sand beneath her feet.

"We must go away," she said.

She held her arms out over the salt, beckoned, and the particles flew around her like dust before a whirlwind, striking her with tiny stinging jabs that touched, stuck to her skin, layered her arms, her neck, her face, with a powder of glistening crystal.

Then she looked once around the room, at the white plaster she had smoothed on the walls, happy, smiling in her fondness, at the fire-scorched white stones in the fire pit, at the white blanket she spread each noon and evening for his return. And she went up the ladder, down again to the edge of the alkali pool.

From the corner of her eye she could see the people coming from the mesa pueblo, their baskets for her salt in their hands. She could tell they were staring with different eyes. But she didn't take any notice of them.

"We are going away," she said to the pool. She bent down, rolled the water surface like a silvery sky-blue blanket, folded it beneath her arm.

Nothing remained where the pool had been but a shallow of mud cleaved with ragged drying cracks.

She began walking away toward the north.

She heard them call her name, but she didn't pause. They had waited too long with their words.

When she reached the foothills, she stopped and looked back at them.

The people were gathered at the depression where her pool had been, some prone on the earth, digging at the dampness for a lingering of salt, some kneeling, licking their own wrists for a residue of salt.

Poor ignorant humans who could not teach their sons faithfulness, who came to her with politeness but no honesty.

She shook her head, saddened at their plight, at her own folly in having loved a young mortal. Then she tucked the alkali blanket more securely under her crystalline arm and turned resolutely toward the north.

THE BUTTERFLY
PURSUIT

The people were at Caliente.
The girl one day saw a beautiful butterfly.
She wanted more than anything to copy the pattern
of the butterfly's wings for her own design.
—OLD PUEBLO MYTH

THERE was no question that she was the finest artisan in the pueblo. And it was obvious that the others looked at her work with the same slightly hurt expression that spread across their faces when they gazed at cactus in purple bloom. Only two hours earlier, she'd been burnishing the delicate rim of a bowl when one of the other village women appeared on her rooftop, had looked at the fragile bowl a long moment, and then had said, her voice vaguely accusing, "My designs will never be that fine."

She shrugged off the residual gloom the woman's words had left and took up the bowl once more. There was nothing she could do about their faintly tearful awe or their uncomfortable regard. She located her polishing stone and hunched back on her heels with the gleaming pebble and the almost finished bowl. She certainly had no intention of releasing one of her bowls for firing that was less than her best. She studied the one in her hands, examined the black borders, the handsome black rabbits mirrored in the center, stark against the white clay. She had no idea what the other woman had seen in her bowl, but she knew it had a perfectly balanced design, perfectly executed. Not a hairline of her yucca brush had swerved aside, not the faintest deviation was discernible between the paired, diamond embossed rabbits. If the other potters in the village were not as practiced, as accomplished, there was nothing she could do about it or about her own talented separation from them.

A movement in the sun hovered at the edge of her sight and she glanced up.

There on the massive heads of the sunflowers just at the line of the roof was a huge black butterfly. It fanned the petals with lazy strokes, wavering and yet remaining essentially motionless, as if it were supported by the thick hot air. It balanced, exposed the minute white veins, the twin translucent white circles on its lower wings.

In its stark black and white it hung, waited, the black wings seeming to hold themselves steady for her scrutiny.

It was the most beautiful thing she'd ever seen.

She carefully replaced the bowl on the roof floor, restraining any abrupt gesture that might frighten the butterfly away.

She had never known there were black butterflies. No one in the pueblo had ever mentioned such a magnificent creature. If only she could capture it and reproduce its white on black exquisite pattern in the center of a new bowl, there would be nothing, no one's art in any village, that could compare to it.

She stretched her hand slowly, slowly, toward it, but it as slowly arched to another sunflower head just beyond her reach.

"I have come." A young male voice called from the ladder. "I have snared two fine hares that your mother can fix for the evening meal."

She recognized Itiwana's voice even before he appeared at the roof.

"Sh-sh-sh," she hissed and motioned him still. But it was too late. The gorgeously arrayed black butterfly circled the sunflowers, descended, fluttered to the street below.

"I thought we could celebrate your new rabbit bowl that...," he began, holding out the brace of animals for approval as he stepped onto the roof.

"My mother is below," she said quickly as she brushed past him and grabbed the ladder poles. She jerked her skirts free and leapt down, trying to keep the great black wings in sight. "I'll be back," she called and then added toward his dismayed face that peered after her, "The rabbits are very fine."

She jumped from the last rung of the ladder and hurried to glimpse the butterfly that had swerved out of sight.

She turned a corner of the pueblo.

There it was, slowly floating down the mesa cliff, black against the sun.

She was running then, letting her sandals cling to the steps chipped in the mesa rock.

As large as a sparrow, the butterfly dipped, swung against the heat, drifted toward the desert floor.

When she returned, she could explain about the butterfly design to Itiwana, soothe away any hurt he might have had at her brusque departure and her lack of appreciation for his hunting prowess. He understood about her work, and he'd often said he was very proud that he was marrying the finest potter in the pueblo. She could even tell him that the butterfly bowl would be her wedding present to him, a gift of art that no one could equal.

The stone path ended and she was in the sand, the grains spraying, flung back from her feet as she ran.

There was the butterfly ahead of her, bobbing, bowing, as if growing from stalks of invisible heat.

She didn't stop to shake the grains of sand from the coils of her sandals but hurried on into the sun.

The black butterfly stayed just ahead of her, tantalizingly near, yet not close enough for her to memorize the design of subtle white against the black.

She thrust her way through outcroppings of yucca, through stunted tangling weeds, into the pueblo's dusty field of corn, and out of the rows once more. And then suddenly she was aware that the black wings with their faint tracings of white were fluttering against a red-orange background, a sunset sky that eased into red-purple and finally faded.

They, she and the beckoning butterfly, had reached a patch of waist-high seed grasses whose heads had faced the west and had drooped with the disappearing sun. The air had become so dark that she could no longer distinguish the silhouette of the equally dark wings, and at last she sank down among the grasses to rest. She was terribly thirsty, and her breath came in loud dry gasps in the black silence.

She put her head down on her drawn-up knees and closed her eyes. But the pattern of the black wings refused to blossom in her mind. She hadn't seen them long enough, well enough to copy them. Not even an outline of the wings would appear behind her eyelids.

She stilled the aching breathing, but the dry constriction in her throat remained. Perhaps the illusive butterfly would be there with the dawn, but perhaps it had flown on blindly in the darkness and she had lost it forever.

She must have slept, for when she lifted her head again, the light in the patch of grass was the yellow-gray of early dawn.

She stood up quickly, stiffly, slightly dizzy. Her knees locked in the morning cold, and she rubbed them as she scanned the yellow-gray masses of seed heads.

The butterfly wasn't there.

A clot of bitterness jammed her throat.

She'd lost it.

After such a long chase, to have come so close, she'd return empty-handed to the village, and she'd never achieve the most beautiful of all bowls.

She'd almost faced back toward the pueblo, when unexpectedly, far ahead, she saw a black speck.

She stared hard into the dawn light.

The black speck was quivering slightly, but it held the air without the movements of bird wings, and she was at once certain that it was the butterfly.

She grabbed a fist-full of grass seeds and stuffed them into her belt as she started running again.

It was so far ahead.

One of her sandals loosened as she raced after the glimmering spot, and she kicked it off without halting, dropped the other as well.

The sharp sand rasped against her bare feet, but she ran on.

At dusk, she realized that her feet had been blistered by the baking earth, but she'd closed the distance of that morning, had come near enough to the butterfly to know that it was in the grove of cedars where she stopped for the night.

She'd find it again when the sun began its climb, and tomorrow she'd catch it.

She sank down against a tree, favoring her burnt soles on the cooling forest mulch.

A rustling came from somewhere behind her.

"Daughter?" a voice whispered from the dark trees.

She shuddered, hugged her knees.

"Daughter, are you there?"

It was a woman's voice, broken with age, whispering from a throat that cracked like a damaged flute.

She waited, but the voice was silent. Finally she said softly, "I am here."

The stirring among the leaves sounded once more.

"I am old," said the frail voice. "I am too feeble to reach a village. I have my grandchild, a tiny baby that cannot be left here among the trees when I can go no farther." There was a pause, as if the voice had to garner strength, and then the old woman went on. "You must take the child with you to the next pueblo."

"No!" She stood up quickly and the pain from her scorched feet throbbed into her calves. "No! I am too close to stop now!" She moved from ear-shot of the voice that hung in the blackness. "I'll return for the baby as soon as I catch the butterfly tomorrow."

She tossed down the grasses from her sash. "Here are some seeds, grandmother. I must go." And she hurried to the edge of the tiny woods, waited without sleeping, listening for sounds that the old woman was following her.

But there was only silence from the forest through the night, and when the first light of dawn paled the sky enough for her to see the black wings, she began to follow them quickly.

She'd catch it soon. Butterflies had a limited life span, that she knew, even wonderful butterflies like the unique black one, but the pattern of the wings wouldn't be altered by death, and when she took up the butterfly, dead or not, she'd go back for the child.

The wings were just ahead.

Yet somehow the shimmering black wings eluded her, always seemed to flutter just beyond her grasp, and her pursuit went on.

She never let it out of her sight, broke her pace only for an occasional sip of tepid water, a bite of cactus fruit, but she lost count of the number of suns that arose, the number of moons that replaced those suns in the night terraced sky.

The chill began earlier in the afternoons, stayed longer during the nights, and she knew that snow would soon layer the sand.

Then one sunrise as she started her quest once more, she came to a barren arroyo protected by a border of spined ocotillo. The butterfly could skim across the sheer rock cliff, but she would have to follow the length of the gulf to find a passage.

She looked in despair across the waste, but she couldn't see the magnificent butterfly in the morning sun.

She ripped off a dangling tatter of her skirt and dropped it on the sand.

Then she stopped and stared down at the ground beside the rag.

There, among the sparse grass, was a dead butterfly, a huge black butterfly.

She nudged it with her foot, spreading the wing span as she turned it over.

Fine white lines branched across the soft black and two translucent white circles dominated the lower wings.

She gazed down at it. It was rather like the one she'd sought so long. But no. It wasn't nearly so spectacular. This one was nice, very pretty in fact, but it would never make the unequalled design in a bowl that the other would make when she copied it.

A sudden wind gusted against her skirt, lifted the brittle wings and swirled them into a forked branch of dry ocotillo where they caught, split, and began to crumble.

But she didn't notice them any longer as she hurried beside the arroyo and searched the empty sky for a glimpse of black wings far ahead.

EAGLE MAN

*The Eagles circled through the sky-hole
until they came to the fifth world.
That was their home.*
—ANCIENT ZUÑI MYTH

HOW do I look?" he asked happily. "Couldn't I be mistaken for an eagle?" He displayed, flapped his arms, and the sewn feathers along the seams of his sleeves rippled like the tips of actual wings.

She looked up from her weaving and smiled. He was such a child in some ways. Her mother had told her she should have called him Eagle Boy, but her mother couldn't help smiling at him as well, at his good humor and his innocence around them, at his enthusiasm for everything on their mountain peak.

"Don't you think I resemble your people more all the time?" he insisted as he leaned over and stroked her cheek.

"I didn't fall in love with you for your resemblance to my people. I want you for my husband just as you are," she said smiling.

"But I think if I covered the entire cloth, if I had a complete shirt of feathers, and then some sort of feathered cap, it wouldn't be as obvious that I'd come from the land below. I'd be more like...."

53

She laughed. "You're just fine." And she gave his hand at her shoulder a brief peck. "But now go below and bring the basket of corn up from the base of the mountain or we won't have anything for the evening meal."

She watched him as he began to climb down the ladder he'd fashioned to ascend and descend their steep rock. His body disappeared below the ledge and he grinned back at her, flailed his arm with the quivering feathers. She smiled again at him fondly, waved him on.

She shook her head as she went back to the careful piece of matting, lacing in the pliant reeds and spun cotton twine so that no air could seep through. She never seemed able to finish anything when he was around with his exuberance, his constant patting and fondling, his constant chatter.

But then he made her life so full of joy that somehow the completion of tasks seemed more frivolous than listening to him and observing him at his constant tinkering. And she continued to smile at the thought of him and his sparkling boyish eyes.

The sun dried the mist hovering at the highest point of the mountains just above their ledge. She looked occasionally at the glimmering snow as she worked. The dazzling snow changed from pale azure to white to palid amber in the ever-altering angles of the sun. But he didn't return.

At last she left her weaving and walked to the edge of their cliff retreat, searched for his shadow on the desert floor far below.

There was nothing.

Her piercing eyes examined each arid bush, each sharpened yucca that she knew so well, but there was no movement, no stirring on the distant sand. And after a while she sighed, went back to work on the woven mat.

What if something had happened to him? He was so trusting that almost anything, anyone, could trap him unaware.

She should never have let him go even to the foot of the mountain alone.

She watched the sun halt at the midsphere of the sky, then invisibly retrace his path as his golden reflection continued on into the descent of the afternoon. In her worried distraction she had to unravel four rows and start again.

The mountains had flattened against the sky, the cone of snow had soaked up the ash of the twilight, and she was visualizing his body smashed in some deep arroyo, the blood on his white buckskins and feathered shirt browning in the dusk, when suddenly his head, quite unbroken or bleeding, appeared above the ledge.

She sprang up and rushed toward him as he swung over the ladder posts onto the rock shelf. "What is it?" She searched his face as she had studied the desert. "Are you all right? Where were you?"

She noted instantly that he was sobered, empty handed, that the eagle feathers of his shirt hung limp at his sides.

"I must talk to you," he said, his face serious, the line of his mouth straight, grim, firm in a way she'd never seen it in all the times he'd returned to their nest from a hunting expedition or foraging in the deserted land below. "Sit here." And he pulled her down beside him near the stone edge.

"What is it?"

He looked at her silently, steadily, for a long moment. "My people are going into battle with the Apaches at dawn," he said finally. "I met them below."

"And you are going to join them?"

There was another pause. His buckskins shown whiter as the light around them dimmed. "I must," he said.

She wanted to urge him not to go, to warn him, but she looked at his determined face and said merely, "When we married, I thought you had changed your loyalty to my people."

He was silent once more for a long time. "Your people are peaceful. My own people are at war, and I must go aid them."

"But once you leave this mountain...," she began, but he stood up, stroked the top of her head.

"I'll be back in a few days time. It will not take long to defeat the Apaches that have come." He climbed down the ladder once again, giving her a reassuring smile as she sat on the cooling stone.

She stayed where she was until he had been gone a long time and the snow on the peak had become as dark as the rest of the mountain.

He was the merriest, the happiest man she'd ever known, the most buoyant and liveliest man who had ever come to the mountain top. But his very endearing childlike qualities were against him, and his beaming innocence kept him from realizing what others, more knowledgeable than he, would have seen, that he could never return to her towering heights once he had rejoined his own people below.

She sighed and rose to go.

She knew the way across the desert even in the blackness, and she was at the mesa of his people well before the center of the night, well before the dawn.

She rested outside the reaches of the firelight, but she could recognize him easily among the clusters of braves despite the rings of ochre with which he had outlined his eye sockets. He had removed the feathered shirt, and a young woman of his own people was barring his chest with stripes of burnt ash paste. He was smiling again.

As she watched from the darkness, she felt the terrible hollow of loss. So that was the real reason he had gone back.

At last the men were ready and they began selecting bows and shields from the pile beside the fire.

She stared into their circle. She wondered if Eagle Man had borrowed weapons or if he had retained his own somewhere in the pueblo of the woman who stood near him and touched his shoulder with her hands, wondered if his own knives and mauls had been shelved in that woman's house against his coming down from the mountain. She watched closely as they left the embers of their bonfire and raced along the trail from the village. The woman ran at his side.

She waited and then followed them from a distance.

She kept his figure in sight as he and the clinging woman and his people plunged prayersticks in the earth, as they shouted a brief chant before the dawn and the Apaches came over the horizon together.

Immediately, arrows, sticks, cries stung the morning sky, and she had to rise to distinguish him among the crush of the others.

There he was, pulling back the bow string with his strong arms that had lifted heaped baskets of corn, that had pried great stones from their settled mountain, that had held her during long snow-thick nights.

She felt the blood in her chest quicken, thud into her throat and head.

And then she saw the atlatl raised against him, the spear aimed, flung at his bare and painted chest.

She swooped without thinking, without considering, and caught his shoulders in her golden talons. She swerved into the air again, pulling him from the battle, from beside the painted girl, from the path of the sharpened oak spear.

The Apache yells followed them as her powerful wings lifted him away, high into the air.

Higher, higher, she soared, until the men and their women were insects far below.

He looked up at her gratefully, smiling. "You came!" he shouted over the beat of the wings. "You came and rescued me!"

She nodded and gazed down at his joyful face. "But you left the eagles and you must now stay with the world of men," she said, as her claws released his shoulders and she let him drop.

THE GIRL WHO HERDED TURKEYS

A long time ago they were dancing
in the winter dance series.
A certain young girl,
not an important girl,
but just an ordinary girl,
went into the kiva to watch.
—ANCIENT ZUÑI MYTH

SHE rubbed their little heads that just fit into her palm, and they nestled their scarlet combs into her hand, arching their necks affectionately against her bare arm. It was a constant surprise to her that in such tiny skulls, the size and shape of green yucca pods, the little brains were able to learn, to know and understand.

But they were. As she curled up on a rock, two of the turkeys snuggled at once on each side of her.

"You're my two sweethearts, aren't you?" she said and stroked their backs, smoothed their feathers.

Their tails flared, fanned open with pleasure, and the white tips shone.

She gazed out across the desert where the rest of the herd preened, paraded, searching among the sagebrush for succulent insects that hadn't yet disappeared into autumn barrows. The turkeys walked delicately around brush and cactus, their angled legs aristocratic as they strolled, dignified even as they hopped upon or over the great rocks that jabbed through the sand crust.

No wonder the people wanted turkey feathers for prayersticks and sacred rituals. The turkeys seemed so wise, and she'd never seen anything more regal, anything lovelier than her herd. She was very proud to have them in her charge, for they were essentially hers, and among all the village people, they came only to her. They needed her, and without her to bring them their parched corn, without her to lead them back to the warmth of the village cages at night, they'd grow thin and die in the winter cold.

But then, she also needed them.

She and her mother were so alone. In their poverty, they were outsiders among the prosperous pueblo women who had husbands, fathers, to bring game. The turkeys were her only friends, her only companions. She'd already acknowledged to herself that she would never marry, that she would be the poor shepherdess of the sacred village turkeys for the rest of her life. There were worse fates, however, and since she was never comfortable in the village, never able even to meet the eyes of any young man of the pueblo, the company of the turkeys was more than enough for her.

And to be able to stay out in the open, to take the turkeys with her, away from the village stares that she knew were constantly probing her shabbiness, was more than recompense for the loneliness she sometimes felt.

The winter months were the loneliest because they were less free, because the village intruded more upon her consciousness. During the coldest days, she had to range close to shelter, to protect the turkeys from the snow, and when she was near, within sight and sound of the village, she could hear rooftop laughter from the other girls her age, occasional fragments of drifted conversations between the girls and young men and her own sharp isolation cut into her contentment with the turkeys.

The thought that winter would soon lock the mesas in iced rigidity lessened her joy in the afternoon. Already the sun was thin, and the graying air was beginning to filter out the heat. Any day she would have to stop close to the pueblo with her herd.

Her feet were slowed as she guided the turkeys back to the village after the sun had disappeared behind the far mountains.

The turkeys seemed to sense her mood, and they clustered around her legs, gazing up at her with their black seed eyes as if to reassure her that they were still there.

She patted their heads rather absently as she closed them in their pens.

"Why don't you go watch the winter dances this evening?" her mother said when they had finished their meal. "You haven't seen the dances in a long time."

It was as if her mother had never noticed how threadbare her skirts had become, as if her mother didn't understand as much as the turkeys with their tiny heads.

"I am tired tonight," she said. "I took the turkeys a long way today to exercise their legs before the cold comes and they cannot stray."

Her mother was waiting for her to add something else and so she said, "Perhaps tomorrow I'll go to the dances in the afternoon."

But as she took the herd far away from the village again the next day, she had no intention of going to the winter dance series. She was simply too out of place and she was much happier among the turkeys who she knew cared for her despite her poverty.

She walked with them, touching, petting them. Then she chose a vantage spot where she could sit and keep watch over them.

The ground was cold as she sat down, the grasses still stiff with the frozen morning dew. She crackled their crystal stems as she stared out beyond the plain.

A turkey came up to her. She reached out to pat him without glancing at him. But instead of plopping down beside her as she'd expected him to do, he leaned over and dropped something from his beak into her lap.

It was a stone.

She picked it up and looked closely at it.

It was a bead, a swirled orange and brown stone that had been shaped, rounded into a polished cylinder, carefully drilled through the center.

"How beautiful," she said, holding the bead up to catch the wan sunlight on its gleaming curves, and the turkey cocked his head at her.

"Thank you, grandfather," she added and put her arm around him. "It is a lovely gift."

When she released him, he cantered away again, stretching his long neck, letting his wings flutter at his plump sides.

She rolled the bead in her hand. The deep worn polish, the length, smooth color, all somehow reminded her of shining turkey quills.

Then all at once the turkey was back, arching his head close to her skirt and dropping something else into her lap.

This time it was a spherical bead of some dark green polished stone, perfectly rounded and drilled from each side for the center hole.

"Where are you finding these lovely beads, little grandfather?"

But the turkey had already loped back to the others in their busy huddle, and she got up to follow him.

The turkeys were on a pebbled rise, scratching, pecking at the stony surface.

"Let's see," she said and bent down among them.

Rain had washed a gash down the side of the little atoll, and she could see sherds of pottery, bits of bone and stone embedded in the water cut.

"It must be a burial place of the Ancient Ones," she said. The turkeys raised their heads and looked at her. "A mound where the Winter People buried their dead before they learned to shelter them in the houses beneath the floors," she added to the turkey's inquiring eyes. "And the beads must have belonged to one of them."

She dropped to her knees and started digging at the dirt slash in the little hill, watching for more beads in the sand, watching for more on the surface where the turkeys were scratching with their yellow toes.

The beads fell from the earth as she dug, beads rose beneath the turkey's claws, and by the time the sun was overhead and her shadow had drawn into a narrow rim at the edge of her skirt, she had a lap-full of the polished stone beads in amber, brown, gold-orange, and green.

"Look, there are enough here for an entire necklace," she said to the turkeys who stood around her. "If I had a string, I could fashion a collar and wear it to the kiva dance this afternoon."

She hadn't known she was going to add that last until she said it.

So she did want to go to the dances after all.

But with a beautiful necklace to wear, she would be as fine as any girl in the village.

One of the turkeys drew close, and a vine fell from his beak onto her skirt.

It was a long trailing vine whose dead leaves had already curled into flaking brown spirals, but the stem itself was still pliant and strong. She could string the beads on it.

"Oh, you sweet, sweet creatures." And she grabbed as many as she could reach, cuddling their yielding warmth, their oily feathers.

Then she began to thread the beads on the vine, selecting, matching, choosing them for a pattern that the original jeweler of the Ancient Ones might have intended.

Her hands shook slightly as she hurried.

When she was finished, she tied the strand at the back and it hung to the curved bones of her throat. She touched it, fondled the smooth coldness of the stones. No one in the entire village had anything so beautiful.

"How do I look?" she cried, and as the turkeys cocked their heads, she joyfully hugged them once more.

"I am going to the kiva dances," she shouted, twirled on her sandals. "Here is corn to keep you happy until I get back. I'll return before sundown to take you back to the pueblo." And she sprinkled some kernels of red and blue corn among the stones on the knoll where it would be easy for them to find.

Then she turned and began to run back toward the village mesa.

One of the older turkeys trotted beside her for a short distance, but as she reached a steep hill, he stopped and gazed after her with his head cocked.

She glanced back at him, then ran on, slowing to a casual walk just before she reached the path up to the rock mesa.

The ancient necklace was heavy at her throat. Her fingers kept straying toward the beads, making her conscious of them, making her hold her head erect to display the beautiful stones.

The kiva was already crowded by the time she came down the ladder and made her way to the adobe benches along the side, but the dancing hadn't yet begun. She saw her mother among the old women at one end, but she didn't join her. Her mother was staring at her with surprise, and she smiled, feeling the necklace at her throat.

Then the dances started and she was drawn instantly into the color, the rhythm, the movement that she hadn't remembered were so powerful.

The first two sets passed without her stirring, almost without her breathing. The kiva fires flared and the drums reverberated in her temples.

There was a gentle touch on her shoulder.

"Would you like to dance the next set with me?"

She looked up startled into the eyes of a young man.

"What?"

"I said, 'Would you like to dance the next set with me?'" He was smiling.

Her hand flew to the necklace.

What a wonderful thing to have a fine piece of jewelry.

He was looking at her admiringly.

"Come. It's just starting." And he grabbed the other hand that was not touching the marvelous beads, led her out into the circle before she had time to think, time to tell him that she hadn't danced since she was a child.

But when the drums began again and the chant echoed from the walls, her feet seemed to remember by themselves, and she smiled and knew she was dancing as well in her necklace as any one of the other village girls.

They danced again and again. And her mind turned only on the rhythm, the flames that whirled and danced with the drums, the young man beside her who kept gazing at her with obvious approval.

"I haven't seen you before," he said as one more set ended.

"Nor I you," she smiled. She'd never looked up to see any young man in the street or at the racing even when she was in the village occasionally, but, of course, she'd spent most of her time away from the pueblo with the turkeys.

She glanced up at the roof square.

It was black.

"Has the sun gone down?" she gasped at him.

"Hours ago, I think." He smiled.

She pulled away quickly and pushed through the crowd of people around the floor.

"Wait! Don't go," he called behind her.

But she was half way up the ladder. And when she emerged onto the roof, she saw that the moon was high in the dark sky.

She heard him on the roof after her as she clambered down the side ladder into the street.

"Wait! I don't even know your name!"

But she didn't pause.

How could she have stayed so long? How could she have forgotten them in the dancing when they were so good, so thoughtful?

Once she tripped over the tangled root of a mesquite and fell headlong, but she scrambled rapidly to her feet again and ran on.

There was the place just ahead.

She could see the mound where they'd found the beads.

She reached it panting, looking around wildly in the moonlight. It was still and empty.

"Here, turkeys, here, turkeys. I have come back."

The moonlight glittered silently on the pebbled mound, on the silvery leaves of the sagebrush.

"I'm sorry I forgot, but I've come back now. Here, turkeys, here, sweet turkeys."

The same gentle touch was at her shoulder, and she turned to see the young man again.

"You're a fast runner. I almost lost you below the last hill."

"They're gone," she said.

"Who?"

"The turkeys." Her voice shook.

"Who?"

"The sacred turkeys." She searched the nearby desert, the dark mountainside. "All of them. The whole herd of beautiful turkeys."

The moonlight shone on the steep distant cliffs, and branched prints seemed to glow in the crags of the rocks, marks across the stone that resembled turkey tracks.

"I forgot them at the kiva dance, and they've.... After they found the beads for the necklace...."

She reached toward her throat, but the necklace was gone. The vine must have snapped and the beads must have scattered as she ran.

Tears spilled over her lids. "It's gone, too. Like the turkeys."

"What is?" He was looking at her with concern and affection in the moonlight.

"The beautiful necklace I was wearing. The one that made you notice me at the kiva and dance with me...."

He touched her shoulder once more. "I didn't realize that you were wearing a necklace," he said. "But if it was dancing with me that made you run and lose it, then it was my fault, and I shall get you another."

His hand moved down her arm until he held her hand again. He smiled, and in the moonlight the creases at the corners of his eyes were shaped like turkey feet.

THE FROG HUSBAND

The people were living at Halonawa.
Many boys wanted to marry the bow priest's daughter,
but she would marry only the young man
who brought the most deer.
—ANCIENT ZUÑI MYTH

VARIANT #1

Y OU must marry," the bow priest, her father, said. "The clan needs your daughters before you are beyond child-bearing age. You must marry within the year."

She didn't look up at her father with his rows of shell necklaces, his wrist-to-elbow bracelets. "I do not love anyone in our pueblo," she said.

He was silent, and even though she still didn't glance up, she knew that he was angry. His bracelets clicked softly like iced grasses against a frozen pond. "Then you will marry someone beyond our pueblo."

And he rose and went down from the roof.

Her mother shook her head. "Now he will make a proclamation and have a dance that will bring young men from other mesas, and it will cost us many prayersticks, many baskets of meal." She scowled into the silver of the morning sun. "Why could you not marry someone from our village?"

"I do not love anyone in our pueblo."

"Fa! What is love?" Her mother spat into the clay to moisten the coils. "Husbands are to bring deer."

She stared into her grinding stone. She had thought about it for so long, had set out so many prayersticks to the kachinas, and perhaps soon she truly would be beyond child-bearing age as her father said. Never to grind the meal for her own husband, for her own family, but always crush the shelled corn for her mother and father. Perhaps the old women were right. Perhaps it was enough to have the deer, the many black and white blankets that a good husband would provide. Perhaps she was foolish to wait any longer.

She ground the meal and thought. At last when the sky began to ripen into the yellow of hot summer gourds, she sighed. "Tell my father that I will marry the man who brings the most deer," she said.

"I will tell him."

The following sunrise, the bow priest decreed before the pueblo that his daughter would marry the young man who brought the most deer.

And the young men began to come.

"How have you lived these days?" each of the young men asked as he laid his deer at her father's feet.

"Happily, thank you," her father answered, and her mother spread the trail of meal from the deer to their house ladder.

There were many young men, and her mother was kept busy laying the road of powdered corn, murmuring to each separate deer, "I am honored that you have come to our house."

But each young man offered only one deer.

Until one day, near sunset, three deer at once were brought.

One of the old women on her roof saw them coming, the three deer, their antlers tangled like branches of tumbleweed, completely obscuring the young man who carried them.

"Look," the old woman called. "Deer for the bow priest's daughter."

And by the time the young man with the deer arrived, the entire pueblo had come to watch, to speculate on the powerful young man beneath the burden who could kill and bring three deer at once.

The deer dropped at her father's feet one at a time, thudding heavily to the earth with their antlers gouging the dust as they crashed to the ground.

A small green frog hopped from beneath the last one.

"I have come to marry your daughter," the frog said politely.

Her father, the bow priest, momentarily gaped down at the frog.

"I have brought three deer and I have come to claim your daughter," the frog said again. His black eyes scanned the gathering of the pueblo and picked her out. He hopped over to her foot. "I have come to marry you."

Her father said quickly before she could speak, said sternly, "It is the proclamation. You are welcome, my son. We will prepare food."

He gestured to her mother who was still staring at the small green frog. "Come! Make the sacred meal road for the deer of our son-in-law."

While her mother attended to the welcome of the deer, the girl went down into the house to prepare the meal cakes. The frog hopped down the ladder after her and perched, the size of a green fist, on the adobe bench of the wall. He watched her lay the fire and nodded his head.

By the time her parents came down the ladder, the meal cakes were ready. Her father carried a tray of dried deer slices.

"Do you...do you eat meat?"

"Yes," said the frog. "My bride will fix a bowl for us and we will eat in the inner room."

"Of course." Her father's shell bracelets clacked like bone dice as he put down the tray.

She filled a bowl with corn cakes, dried meat, and went into the other room. She could hear the frog hopping behind her on the hard adobe floor, hopping with soft moist plops behind her.

She put the food on the ceremonial white blanket while the frog watched her.

"Why did you stipulate that your bridegroom would be the one who brought the most deer?"

She heard her voice near a shallow of tears. "I thought it might be enough that a husband provide deer as the old women in the village say."

He looked at her from beneath his puckered green lids and lifted a corn cake between his narrow webbed feet. "It's not enough," he said.

VARIANT #2

THE bow priest's daughter could find no groom that suited her among the pueblo. All of the young girls her age married before her, even the demanding Shakala who at last married a plump young man with fringing hair who had brought her parents a dozen black and white blankets in payment for her hand.

The night of Shakala's wedding, the bow priest's daughter dreamt that she was one of the old women of the village, dressed in a plain black blanket and her hair still in maiden whorls. She had no sons, no grandchildren around her. No one was near to listen to the words that came from her dream mouth.

In the morning, the girl remembered the dream and told her father that she had decided to marry the young man who brought the most deer.

But the young man who brought three deer and won her hand was a small green frog, and the girl was ashamed before the village and Shakala. It was the proclamation of the bow priest, however, that she would marry the one who brought the most deer, and she had to prepare a meal for her bridegroom and go with him into the separate room of the house.

As she went into the room and the blanket of the doorway fell shut, she glanced back over her shoulder.

A handsome young man in white buckskins and many turquoise necklaces stood in the room. The tiny fire flickered and gleamed across his tall lithe form.

"Where is the frog?"

The handsome young man looked down at her. "I am your frog husband," he said. "Did you think an ordinary frog could have brought three deer?"

She held out the bowl of corn balls and he sat down beside her. He was very handsome and slim and his hair was plaited in long sleek braids. She looked at him and was glad that he had brought the most deer.

Shakala would be pierced with envy when she saw him beside her own new fat bridegroom.

"Is it the custom among your people for the couple to be betrothed if they spend the night together, apart from parents?"

She nodded.

"Good," he said and took another of the corn cakes.

She watched him eat and took small bites of her own fresh corn balls. She wondered if that was what the old women knew, that if a man had prowess, were a fine hunter and provider, he would be handsome and make a good husband. She wanted to ask him, but he seemed so wise that she didn't want to appear ignorant. Of course she should have known that the frog with the three deer was no ordinary frog.

When the little hearth fire fell into orange embers, she gave him a newly woven blanket and they rolled up separately, but near each other. In the morning they would be betrothed.

She had trouble sleeping and had dreams she couldn't remember when she awoke. But each time she looked beside her, she saw the handsome young man asleep, and she smiled as she thought of how jealous Shakala would be.

"It is morning," her father's voice came through the doorway blanket.

The young man helped her up and they went together into the other room. Her mother and father stared speechless, and she was pleased. She knew that the whole pueblo would stare when they saw him.

"We will announce the betrothal," her father said in his calm bow priest voice, but she knew he wanted to ask about the frog. She knew he was as stunned as her mother by the appearance of the new son-in-law.

They went up the ladder to the roof with her father. The sun had turned the sky to white bone and the mesas were already golden.

"I will find a runner to bring the pueblo together," her father said and went down into the square before their house.

She and the young man stood on the roof side by side. It was good to have her future assured, she thought, good to have found a husband who would be not only a good hunter but who was very handsome as well.

She gazed at him proudly.

But in the fierce glare from the cloudless white sky she noticed that there was a faint green tint to his eyelids.

KACHINA TWILIGHT

*The Kachinas, when they are killed,
become deer and go into the land of the
undying ancients.*
—ANCIENT ZUÑI MYTH

THE surprisingly severe birth pains
had left her weak. She lay back on the fresh blanket, wiped the thick
sweat from her upper lip. The old women hadn't told her it would be
so painful.

She glanced across the room to where they were washing the baby
with yucca suds, sprinkling the floor with sacred meal. They should
have told her. She raised herself slightly on her elbows to watch them
in the firelight.

"Ah, you have a fine big girl here," one of the old women looked
up from the baby and said in her dry crow voice. Her spidery head
nodded, bobbed happily. "She will be a lovely bride, will bring a fine
husband into the clan."

The clan. The clan. That was all any of the old people ever thought
about. As if there were nothing else important on the mesas of the
brown earth but the precious clan. She didn't answer the old voice
and turned over on her side facing the adobe wall. They could at least
have warned her that the baby would cut her inside like sharp honed
flint as it tore loose.

The old women went on talking to each other, praising the baby's sturdy fist and legs, bundling it in the rabbit fur robe she had worked so hard to fashion, stripping, twisting the hide around the fique strands.

It wasn't fair. All they cared about was the clan.

Her husband had sisters who had already birthed their quota of babies for his clan, but he hadn't said anything about their pain. He had just kissed her and then hurried off to the kiva, leaving her with the grandmothers and their hoarse bird tongues, their shriveled bird talon hands that had clawed at her flesh from the outside while the ripping of the baby sliced her from within.

"Here, here." One of the ancient hands smoothed back her hair, wiped her forehead. She wanted to jerk away, push the old nails out of reach, but she controlled her muscles, her nerves, and as the croak of the ancient woman said, "Here, drink this tea," she lifted her head, obediently took the warmed swallows held to her lips.

She was instantly so tired that she had to close her eyes and sink into the blanket. She continued to hear the old bird women in the room, continued to hear the pop of the greasewood branches in the rock-lined hearth, but her eyelids were so heavy that she lacked the strength to pry them open.

When she did open her eyes again, sunlight dropped in a thick yellow shaft through the roof square, and she knew it was noon.

"Ah, you are awake, daughter." One of the wrinkled grandmothers was peering down at her, close to her face. "Your husband has been waiting long to see you."

She wasn't sure she wanted to see him. She wasn't sure how she felt about him. He had gone to the kiva and had left her with the pain all alone.

But somehow she didn't know how to say that to the creased faces of the old women, and she let them dress her, arrange her hair, without protest. And when they helped her to her feet, she was unsteady, but surprised to find that the pain had almost disappeared.

"Come along, daughter. Your husband must be getting impatient." The old crones surrounded her at the ladder poles and she was forced to climb up toward the roof.

When she reached the open square into the noon sun, she saw her husband at the edge of the roof, but she didn't look at him and instead reached for the baby that her grandmother had carried up the ladder behind her.

She felt him approach, stand beside her shoulder, as she kept her eyes on the baby.

"I am very proud of you," he said softly. "They have told me that you were brave in the childbirth, but I knew you would be."

She glanced into his face.

His eyes were glittering with pride and love.

She leaned back against him, and as his arms enfolded her, she suddenly felt very secure and blissful. "We have a girl," she said.

"Yes." And his arms were tight around her.

They stood a moment, the three of them in the sun. Then they sank down together on the roof floor and put the baby on their laps.

"Isn't she beautiful?"

He smiled at her, the pride brimming in his eyes, on his glowing cheeks. "A child of yours would have to be."

"The grandmothers spoke of how glad the clan will be." She said it tentatively, her first clear testing of it in her own throat.

"Of course. The clan must have such fine daughters to bring in more men, to make the people prosper. Like you did when you caught me," he said, teasing her cheek with his fingers.

She caught his hand before he could move it away and kissed the palm.

"We will watch her grow strong and sturdy, marry, and have more daughters who will have more daughters, and the clan shall spread to all the land we see from here."

How peaceful it was, how soothing his words. She pressed herself against him, the baby in its light cradle between them, and watched the late afternoon sun replace the hot noon one.

"We must go down soon to the kachina dance in honor of our child," he said at last.

She nodded. "Soon."

It was as if the evening had stopped in the lavender of the sky, as if her night of travail had happened years earlier, and now their days and generations stretched out before them on the plains, the clan around them endless, peopling the myriad of stern mesas beyond their pueblo.

It was so calm.

Then he sat up straighter beside her. "Look," he said and pointed toward the south.

A strange procession was making its way slowly across the grasslands. Many beings that seemed half man, half some animal, possibly antelope but not quite, were glittering in the fading sunlight.

"Kachinas," she said, and they got up and went to the edge of the roof to watch.

"It is only fitting that new kachinas should appear for the kachina dance of our child," he said and smiled, but she knew he half meant it.

He took her hand and they watched the parade of kachinas come closer.

Only gods could be so arrayed, only princely kachinas from the south where the goddess of the jade skirt reigned could appear so magnificent.

And then she could distinguish other beings that had the shape of men walking beside the half animal ones, all of them wearing helmets, masks, breastpieces that shone with the force of obsidian mirrors. The almost antelopes without horns but with a second man head moved daintily through the grasses, between the corn rows of their village fields below. Silver, burnished copper, turquoise, shell, and coral. They shone with every precious thing as they filed ever nearer.

She waited, holding his hand tightly, wondering if he too felt the awe she recognized in herself.

Finally the procession reached the foot of their mesa, and the kachina slightly in front of the others looked up, seemed to be gazing directly into her eyes.

"I am Don Francisco Vasquez de Coronado," he shouted up toward them and swept his arm in the motion of a lake wave. "I hereby claim this land, this mesa, and these Seven Cities of Cibola in the name of King Carlos V of Spain."

PHOTO BY AMY WILSON

PAT CARR was born in Grass Creek, Wyoming, but spent most of her life in Texas. She has received wide recognition for her writing, including a South and West Fiction Award, a Marc IV Library of Congress Award, a National Endowment for the Humanities, the Iowa Short Fiction Award, a Green Mountain Short Fiction Award, and the Texas Institute of Letters Short Story Award.

Pat Carr's other books are *The Grass Creek Chronicle*, 1976; *Bernard Shaw*, 1976; *The Women in the Mirror*, 1977; *Mimbres Mythology*, 1979; *Night of the Luminarias*, 1986; and *In Fine Spirits*, 1986. She has a collection of short stories, *American Stories*, in press with the University of Arkansas Press.

Pat and her family currently live in New Orleans, where she teaches at the University of New Orleans.

◄ *Pat Carr with her dogs, Faulkner and Behn*

The cover and book design is by
Vicki Trego Hill of El Paso, Texas.

•

The type is Paladium and is set by
Camille of El Paso, Texas.

•

Special thanks to Chuck Sullivan.

EL PASO • TEXAS